ISBN: 9798755036535

Also, by Frances Everly:

Wishing on Snowflakes

<u>Love Born of Fire Trilogy</u>

Hawk's Heart

Piper's Promise

Dreaming of Deacon

Coming in 2022

Broken by the Devil

Books written as F.D. Everly

The Phoenix and Fae (2022): Book 1 of The Phoenix Crown Saga

Bardon's Curse (2022): A novella from The Phoenix Crown Saga

Dedicated to my dad, who will thankfully never read this book, but who has always supported my writing and my dreams.

Thank you, Dad!

Dreaming of Deacon

Prologue

Pain seared along the length of his body, causing him to gasp as he struggled to cling to consciousness. The acrid smell of smoke was coming from somewhere nearby, infecting his lungs and making him cough. Shouts and rapid gunfire echoed through the streets. A bullet slammed into the brick wall behind him, inches away from his head, sending dust and pieces of stone cascading over him. Somehow, he managed to drag his body over broken glass and sharp rocks scattered across the ground to shelter behind the burnt husk of a car. More bullets ricocheted off the twisted scraps of metal that had once been part of his convoy. Deacon squeezed his eyes closed, thinking of his friends, and prayed they found cover somewhere nearby. He wasn't a religious man, but if there were ever a time to have a little faith, he decided this would be it. He sent up another quick prayer to find a way out of this mess.

It was supposed to be a simple supply run for the schools they were building nearby. None of the recon had suggested a hint of rebel soldiers anywhere within the vicinity. How the hell had this happened? He winced, searching the ground for a weapon of any kind. With no hint as to the enemy's whereabouts, he had no clue how he was going to get out of this and rejoin his unit… if there was a unit to rejoin. He squashed the sudden despairing visions that seared through his brain, blinking back the dots that started clouding his vision. He slumped to the ground, his legs giving out beneath him. Who was he kidding? Injured, and alone in enemy territory without a weapon of any kind… he was a dead man. He might as well give up and pray his injuries claimed him before the enemy did.

"Move! Get your ass off the ground Deacon! It's not safe out here! Move it! Now! Get up!"

A familiar voice screamed in his ear. He wanted to look around for the source, a sliver of hope that someone from his unit had survived blooming in his gut, but the blackness seemed so welcoming and promised an escape from the pain. The screaming voice shrieked in his ear again and demanded he fight the blackness, over and over, an order coming from a broken record.

"Get up Deacon! Move! Don't give up! You need to get up and move! NOW!" It screamed. "You're not safe here! MOVE! MOVE! MOVE!"

Deacon smiled. The voice sounded like his grandfather, Travis. He missed his grandfather's orneriness and meddlesome tactics. Travis was always up to something, or busy with the farm. Ever since Grandma Mary passed away from an aggressive form of breast cancer right after Deacon had graduated from High School, Travis found new ways to keep himself busy. Like the time he'd decorated the orchard for Hallowe'en and invited the entire town out for a good scare to raise money for research. A couple of Deacon's friends had needed a change of clothes afterwards, but no one thought twice about teasing them for it. His best friend Charlie had grown out his beard after that, convinced it would make him seem more manly after screaming like a little girl and running out of the orchard with a bloody zombie, gore dripping from his chin and gaping wounds on his belly, chasing after him. Alex, his stepfather, and a famous actor had helped with hiring the actors and finding the special effects team that had played a big part of pulling the entire thing off. But it had all been Travis's idea. That was the best Hallowe'en

Deacon had ever had. He wished he was home now, making plans for another "Haunted Forrest" instead of here in the middle of a deserted town that had once housed hundreds of people, barely clinging to consciousness as another explosion rocked the ground beneath him.

The brick wall behind him swayed back and forth, threatening to collapse on top of him. Somewhere to his left he could hear shouts coming closer and the voice in his head was screaming at him, louder now and increasingly relentless. It was impossible to ignore, and the louder it got, the more that blissful darkness seemed to fade, until it was completely out of his grasp. Groaning, he struggled onto his feet, gasping at the sharp stabs of pain in his side. Closing his eyes, he let out a pained hiss and assessed the situation. He was lucky his body armour seemed to have born the brunt of the initial attack, but a piece of shrapnel was sticking out of his side and his uniform was still smoking. Grasping the jagged piece of metal, he fought the urge to pull it out of his body, clenching his teeth to keep from screaming as pain tore through him with every little movement. He didn't know much about injuries like this, but he decided the damage the shrapnel would do to his body while he tried to escape the attack couldn't be worse than bleeding out because of his own stupidity in yanking the damn thing out. Dots clouded his vision as he struggled to stand and promptly collapsed on the ground, panting from the exertion, and fighting against the abyss that threatened to consume him.

"MOVE NOW!" The voice demanded. "MOVE, MOVE, MOVE!"

Blinking the sweat out of his eyes, he surveyed his surroundings, searching for a way to escape quickly before he was discovered by the wrong people. His gaze fell on a sewer grate, partially hidden beneath the debris. The sound of gunfire was getting closer, forcing him to make a quick decision and he dragged himself towards the grate, gritting his teeth to keep from making a sound.

Once he reached it, he paused to catch his breath, before grasping the bars and yanking as hard as he could. Pain tore through his body, spots dotting his vision once more. He kept pulling on that grate until, with a screech of metal on stone, it gave way. The suddenness of its release caused him to fall backwards before he managed to regain his balance.

Pressing a trembling hand to the wound in his side, he stared at the hole in the ground. It seemed awfully small, and he wondered if he could fit his large frame through that tiny opening. A cursory glance around the street revealed there was nowhere else for him to hide. Injured and weaponless, he was a sitting duck out here in the open. He had to at least try to squeeze inside. It was his only chance.

"Don't stop now. You're almost there!"

Ignoring the stomach-churning smells that escaped from below, he slowly eased his legs and then his body inside. Lowering himself into the depths below, he unsteadily landed on his feet with a splash, wavering for a moment as he fought to remain upright. Something skittered across his foot. Choking back the bile that rose in his throat, he waited for his eyes to adjust to the sudden darkness before he began wading his way through the sewer, hoping to get as far away from the scene of battle above as he could, and rejoin his men.

As he ran, he decided it was time to return home. No betrayal was worth all of this. He'd avoided seeing his stepfather long enough. Once upon a time he'd admired the man that had fallen in love with his mother and taught him to play guitar. He hated that he'd kept this secret, letting it eat away at him for ten years and keeping him away from his farm and his family. His mother would be devastated, of course. That was the whole reason he'd chosen to keep it to himself. Her first husband had abused her and cheated on her frequently. It wasn't fair that she was going to have to deal with the infidelity of yet another man. She deserved better, and so did Deacon. It was his fault that he'd introduced Alex to the temptress that was Deacon's ex-girlfriend. His fault that his entire family was going to be destroyed from this betrayal, but he couldn't continue to stay away anymore. Not after this. He wanted to go home to the farm, where no one was shooting at him. He wanted to die an old man amongst the orchard blossoms, not a man in his prime, fleeing a battle in a sewer where no one would ever find his rotting corpse. Alex needed to face what he'd done and take responsibility for the child he'd given another woman. The child that Deacon had been supporting for ten years. If he got out of this sewer, Deacon was going home.

Chapter 1

Now

*"I used to dream of bigger things than being a farmer.
Everything changed the day I laid eyes on Rose." -Travis's
journal*

"Brainstorming people. I need ideas for our next great script!
What have you got for me?" Amaira watched Darrell's jowls
jiggle as he shouted excitedly to everyone gathered around the
long table in the studio's board room. Darrell Jones was one of
the top producers in the film making industry, and she was
excited for the opportunity to work with him and Film Hawk
Productions. After working hard in college to get her degree in
screenwriting and spending her summers as an unpaid intern for
various production companies, this was her big break. No more
coffee runs and mail delivery. This was it. This was her chance to
show everyone what she could do. She didn't want to blow it on
her first day, but she was woefully unprepared for an intense
brainstorming session. She tapped her pen on the yellow legal
pad in front of her and wracked her brain for ideas, at the same
time hoping someone else would come up with a great idea and
she could sit quietly in the back and observe.

"Alien films are always a hit," Andre Parsons, one of the
senior script writers with the production company, blurted out

from where he sat near the door. "Great opportunities for action and horror."

"And the industry is saturated with them!" A well-dressed woman with curly black hair and dark skin shouted, shooting down Andre's idea before he had the chance to continue his pitch. "We should be doing something new, something fresh. What about an inner-city romance? There's plenty of opportunities to give audiences something to root for."

"Inner-city films have been done to death lately. There's nothing new and fresh about them," Darrell ruthlessly shot down the woman's idea, shaking his head and sending his jowls flying again.

Amaira anxiously bit her pen, her gaze landing on one of the other producers and the owner of Film Hawk. Her boss Xander Hawkins was a brilliant actor, with multiple awards lining his resume. She'd been a huge fan since she was in middle school, and like many girls she knew, she'd been heartbroken when he'd settled down and gotten married. Now he was a father of three, and still happily married seventeen years later. From what she remembered, his early relationship with his wife had been something of a hot topic for a couple years. Something to do with a crazy, stalker ex-girlfriend of his catching them in bed together in Mexico. She idly jotted down what she could remember after all these years. He'd met his wife in Mexico after *Bonnie and Clyde* went into post-production, and he'd publicly broken up with his co-star. Amaira wracked her brain for the woman's name but couldn't think of it. In fact, she couldn't remember another movie the woman had been in since.

"Damn," she whispered under her breath, staring at her notes when someone coughed. She looked up and realized that every pair of eyes were resting on her.

11

"Are we interrupting something?" Darrell demanded, staring at her pages of notes.

"Oh, no. Sorry. I didn't mean to be rude." She stammered, hoping no one would notice her flaming cheeks. She took a deep breath and blurted out her pitch, the only thing she could come up with on the fly, and prayed she wasn't about to lose her job on her first day. She didn't want to go back to being a freelance writer while working in her mother's dance studio to pay the bills. She absolutely hated ballet, but she'd never admit it to her mother, a retired prima ballerina with the New York Ballet Company.

"What about a romantic documentary?" She pitched anxiously; her voice barely audible. "From what I remember, Mr. Hawkins's romance with his wife was hot news back in the day, and he remains one of the hottest stars in the industry."

Amaira held her breath as she looked around the eerily silent room. Andre looked from her to Xander and back again, and she half expected him to fire her on the spot. She couldn't tell what Xander was thinking, his eyes boring into her with a hard look in them that made her wish she could melt through the floor and move to some backwoods town far away from Hollywood's reach. But even with the sound of blood rushing in her ears, she reminded herself that this is what she signed up for. Nothing worth having was easy, and she desperately wanted to fork out a career as a screenwriter, not a ballet teacher.

"I like it," Darrell announced, cutting through the thick silence of the room. "It's romantic and steamy enough to fog up the big screen-."

"No," Xander's voice was full of ice as he protested. "My wife went through hell because of all that press. I refuse to put her and my family through it again!"

"Xander, come on. It would a documentary for the ages! Think about all the awards and recognition you could-." Darrell began to plead with Xander, but he simply shook his head and cut him off.

"Not a chance, Darrell!" He responded coldly, standing forcefully enough to send his chair flying into the wall behind him.

"How about we change it?" The curly haired woman pitched in. "Your wife grew up on a farm, right? Well, how about we change it from a documentary to a Country Romance? Use the real story to inspire a new one?"

Xander grunted, but Amaira could feel the atmosphere of room relax, as if everyone were taking a collective sigh of relief that he hadn't fired them all and stormed out of the room.

"I still don't like it," he muttered grudgingly. "You can use our story to inspire something new. I'll give you two months to come up with a script. If I like it, we'll use it. If not, you can all forget the whole damn thing."

"A country… romance?" Amaira squeaked. "I don't know anything about farms."

Darrell looked from Amaira to Xander with a grin on his face that made Amaira wish she could be a fly on the wall in that man's brain right now. She wondered if that grin meant she should be worried, and then she discovered a few minutes later exactly what he was thinking.

"Your in-laws have a farm, Xander. What better place than that for our script writers to live and learn the life of a farmer, and of the famous Xander Hawkins?" Darrell pitched, tapping his fingers on the table.

"I'll discuss it with my wife. In the meantime, keep brainstorming!" Xander growled reluctantly before stalking out of the room and leaving Amaira gaping at the closed door. She couldn't believe it. Her pitch had worked, but now she was going to be expected to learn about farming. Where was his in-laws farm?

"Well, new girl, pack your bags. As soon as my secretary can make the arrangements, you will be heading to Canada." Darrell chuckled, standing, and following Xander out of the board room at a more relaxed, almost gleeful pace.

~⚬~

"Canada? I don't understand why you have to go so far to write a script," Vivienne exclaimed, exasperation evident in her tone. "You're going to miss your father's award ceremony that his work is hosting. Remember? It's all he's been talking about for weeks."

Amaira sighed and pinched the bridge of her nose. She knew what a big deal it was that the pharmaceutical company her father worked for his entire adult life was hosting a lifetime achievement award dinner to honour his work on cancer research. The whole evening was a black-tie event with special tributes to his work and dedication to his research. Her brother, Hamir, was even coming from Colorado for it and bringing his entire family.

She'd been looking forward to his visit for weeks, and now she'd be lucky if she made it back in time to spend anytime with them.

"I know Mama. If I could delay this trip somehow, I would. I had no idea that my pitch would have any traction at all, let alone lead to a trip to another country," she apologized for the tenth time since sitting down for lunch.

"Is there nothing you can do to get out of it?" Vivienne pleaded, ignoring the waiter as he arrived with their appetizers.

"I'm sorry Mama. The producers want the script written where the romance between the famous Xander Hawkins and his wife fell in love. It'll be more authentic that way, I guess. I'll also be spending a lot of time with him and his family there, for character research. I want to be at the gala for Papa so badly, but this script could make or break my career before it even begins. Papa would understand if he were here," Amaira thanked the waiter and spread a cloth napkin over her legs. She loved her mom, and having been a hugely successful ballerina, one would think she would understand her daughter's drive to be involved and successful in the film industry. Still, she really didn't want to miss her father's big night. She was upset that she'd have to miss it.

"I suppose you're right," Vivienne finally relented, taking a sip of her red wine. "He has always said 'Having dreams is great, but you have to work hard to achieve them.'"

"I never realized how cheesy that sounded before," Amaira snorted.

"Still… Canada? I thought they fell in love in Mexico. It's so cold up there this time of year. Couldn't they send you somewhere tropical instead?" Vivienne asked.

"They did... or at least they fell in lust there. Xander explained that it wasn't until he'd spent time with his wife on her family farm that he realized he loved her. Besides, he doesn't want to re-enact the scandal that ensued when Marissa Tate invaded his privacy and his hotel suite," Amaira explained, remembering the discussion she'd had with him in his office after he'd calmed down and apologized for being defensive about his family. She doubted there were many A-list actors who would bother, and it confirmed for Amaira how nice and down to earth he was.

"Marissa who?" Vivienne innocently batted her lashes. "Oh, was she the actress who publicly announced their engagement and then walked into his suite while he was having sex with-."

"Sarah Mackenzie," Amaira supplied. "Yep, she's the one that nearly broke him and his wife apart before their relationship even had a chance."

"Ah. Alright then, I think I understand it all now. Just be sure to pack a lot of warm clothing. Frostbite can be nasty on your toes, and you'll need those if you want to keep dancing," Vivienne advised.

"I'm not going to the arctic, mama," she laughed, washing down her salad with a glass of sparkling water. "And if Papa's upset, just remind him that his beloved older son, Hamir, will gladly be there with his wife and their entire brood of offspring to make up for it."

"Amaira, that's no way to talk about your brother. You know your father loves you both equally," Vivienne admonished, waving her fork around.

"I know," Amaira sighed, stabbing at a stray piece of lettuce. "But Hamir understands Papa's research, at least, since he followed Papa's footsteps. I'm completely clueless about alleles

16

and genomes and all that DNA stuff they're always talking about. I always feel like I need to pinch myself awake when they start with their geek-speak. There's a reason you and I are besties, you know."

"You're not alone, darling," Vivienne laughed, her green eyes crinkling as her entire face lit up, her auburn locks catching in the breeze. Once famed for her classic Irish beauty, despite being a native New Yorker, and talent for the New York Ballet Company. Her mother was still a great beauty, Amaira reflected with a smile, and hoped she would look as youthful as her mother when she was that age. Even if she did inherit her father's black hair and brown eyes, at least she'd inherited her mother's high cheekbones and alabaster complexion to make up for it. "I was nearly comatose by dinner last Christmas. I'm grateful that at least one of my children followed my footsteps and is engaging in the arts. Though I had hoped you would become a ballet dancer or act on Broadway."

"Not everyone was meant for the spotlight, Mama. Dancing was your thing, writing is mine. C'est la vie," Amaira shrugged.

"So, when do you leave again?" Her mother asked, settling the bill, and gathering her purse and sunglasses.

"The day after tomorrow. I'm flying out of LAX and should land in Toronto by dinner time," Amaira answered, relieved to finally be finished with lunch and this conversation.

Chapter 2

"The first time I saw Rose, she took my breath away. Her hair glowed in the sun as if lit with a halo, and she laughed at me when I said so. I knew then that we were destined to be together. It was only a matter of time before she saw it too." -Travis's journal

Amaira pulled to a stop in front of a quaint, but ancient farmhouse. She still couldn't believe her first assignment had her travelling so far away from Los Angeles. Or that she would be staying with Xander's family on their farm while she wrote. She tapped her fingers on the steering wheel of her rental car as she took in her surroundings. The garden had a wild sort of beauty that served to accent the stone porch and the grey two-story house. Off to her right was an old barn, and another building that was surrounded by vehicles. She remembered through her quick research of the place that there was a small store or market on the property that offered local produce and artisan products, and likely other things as well. Yet another place on her list of areas to explore while she was here.

Grabbing her purse from the passenger seat, she carefully climbed out of the car and stretched before heading up the steps to the house. She raised her fist to knock when she heard raised voices coming from inside. It sounded like multiple people were talking at once. Were they having a party? She didn't want to intrude. She decided to come back later. Amaira was halfway down the porch steps when the front door suddenly flew open. A tall, gorgeous Adonis of a man stood in the doorway, his large frame nearly filling the entire space.

Amaira sucked in a startled breath. Her tongue thickened in her mouth as she salivated over the sight in front of her. Heat burned from the roots of her hair all the way down to her toes and she completely lost the ability to do anything beyond gape at the man. In the years that she had lived in Los Angeles, and worked with some of Hollywood's handsomest men, never had one affected her in such a way. His blue eyes bore through her, sending butterflies fluttering in her stomach and making the hair on the back of her neck stand on end. His short, golden-brown hair fell rakishly over his eyes, and she had a strong urge to run her fingers through it and brush it out of his face.

"Can I help you? Or did you just come to stare at me?" He asked, his deep voice rumbling through her, shaking her to her core.

"I-I wasn't staring," she stammered and grimaced. That's exactly what she had been doing and her cheeks burned with embarrassment. She refused to be intimidated by him, however, and steeled her spine before continuing.

"I'm Amaira Devan. I'm a screen writer for Film Hawk Productions. I didn't mean to intrude on your festivities, I was to believe that you would be expecting me. I must be at the wrong address. I'll give Mr. Hawkins a quick call. I'm so sorry for intruding. I believe I saw a Bed and Breakfast on my way through town, I'll stay there until I can sort things out with my boss. Sorry to have disturbed you." She turned back towards her car and quickly started down the remaining steps. He muttered something under his breath that she didn't quite catch, and she wasn't entirely sure that she wanted too. Her hands shook as she searched her purse for her keys, groaning when they weren't on top like they should have been since she'd only put them in there a few minutes ago. A gentle hand on her arm stopped her with its strong grip, and she looked up to see that he had followed her.

"I'm sorry I was so rude. It's been an emotional day for all of us and your arrival caught me off guard. Xander mentioned you would be coming, but I think my homecoming has thrown everyone for a loop. It was rather sudden. I'm Deacon," he introduced himself, the heat from his strong hand burning through the thin fabric of her sleeve.

"Deacon?" she asked, wracking her brain for any mention of him.

"Deacon Mackenzie. I'm Xander's stepson," he answered, shoving his hands into his pocket.

"Of course. Mr. Hawkins mentioned that you were serving overseas in the military." She remembered Xander mentioning it in passing.

"I was," he responded with a shrug of his broad shoulders. "Do you have any bags? I'll bring them in for you. I think my mom has had a room ready for you since Xander brought up the whole movie thing."

"That's alright. I don't want to be a bother," she waved him off. "I'll just get a room at the Bed and Breakfast. Don't worry about me. Please, go enjoy your party."

"If my being here makes you uncomfortable at all, I can sleep in the barn," he teased, grinning. "My mother would kill me if I sent you away. Come on, I'll show you where you're going to be staying while you're here."

Deacon took the keys from her hand and opened her trunk before she had a chance to refuse again. She bit her tongue irritably and watched as he started pulling her bags out with an ease that she wished she'd had when she had struggled to drag them through the airport. She hated being strong-armed, but she needed this job, and she didn't want to offend her boss's family by refusing their hospitality. Deacon turned his grin on her again, making her insides quiver as he sauntered by with her duffle bag slung over his shoulder and a suitcase in each hand.

"Welcome to my farm." He said as he passed. "Welcome to Mackenzie Orchards."

Chapter 3

"I convinced my parents to hire Rose in the market for the summer. I know they needed the extra help. Plus, it helped keep her close while I figured out how to talk to her like a normal person. Whenever she was around, I always said the dumbest things. It was like I forgot how to speak or something." -Travis's journal

Amaira was mortified to be paraded through a house full of strangers by a man who's name she'd only just learned. Her father would be horrified if he were there to witness it. He might had married a modern American woman, but he still had a strong sense of traditionalism and honor. She didn't tell him half the stuff she got up to because of it. She was far from being a saint, but at least she tried to be discreet about it. Being the center of attention had never been enjoyable to her, and she hated having all those eyes on her. What must they be thinking? By the time they reached what would be her room for the next month or more, she was furious with Deacon for putting her through that. Why couldn't he have let her find a room at the Bed and Breakfast?

"Why couldn't you let me leave?" she demanded, crossing her arms over her chest as she followed him into the guest bedroom. Deacon's eyebrows shot up in surprise as he glanced at her standing in the doorway before resuming his task of placing her bags on the bed.

"Why should you need a room somewhere else when this one's already yours? Over there you even have a private bathroom," he pointed in the direction of a door next to the closet, frustrating her further. "It doesn't have a shower though, so you'll have to share the one down the hall. I'll give you a tour of the rest of the house and farm once your settled. You must be exhausted after that flight. We can talk in the morning or later tonight after everyone leaves. You're welcome to come down and grab a bite to eat or mingle if you'd like."

"I'd prefer to make my own choices, not have someone parade me through a room full of people who stared at me as if I were some sort of curiosity! I hate being the center of attention." She explained, irritated by his disregard of her wishes.

Without another thought, Amaira turned and marched out of the room, desperate to find a private place where she could calm her nerves before she made a complete fool of herself. After a few seconds she could hear Deacon's heavy footsteps behind her as she made her way down the stairs. At the bottom she barely stopped herself from crashing into another woman. Her lavender eyes widened at the sight of her and the man a few steps behind her.

"Piper, meet Amaira," Deacon introduced her. "She's the writer that Xander mentioned would be staying with us for awhile."

Amaira pasted the cheeriest smile she could muster on her face and held out her hand. The other woman was beautiful and very blonde, and despite herself, Amaira wondered if she was Deacon's lover. She cringed at the jealousy that roared through her chest and prayed the smile on her face hadn't become strained with that ugly and senseless emotion. Why should she care who Deacon took to his bed? They'd barely met, and he'd already proven that a swarm of mosquitoes was less irritating.

"It's lovely to meet you," she said instead of asking the question that screamed in her mind. Their relationship was none of her business, she reminded herself. She was here to do a job and then she would be back in Los Angeles before the end of summer. Sooner if she was lucky.

"Amaira, what a pretty name," Piper smiled warmly as she gently shook her hand. "Welcome to the farm. I hope my stepson hasn't completely forgotten his manners. He can be a little dense sometimes. Takes after his father."

Amaira chuckled and refused to examine the sense of relief that coursed through her heart. She'd forgotten that Xander's wife had been young when she'd had her first child. Barely nineteen and already married to her first husband, whom Amaira assumed must be Piper's husband if she was Deacon's stepmother. It struck her as odd that Piper would be in Mrs. Hawkins' childhood home, but then she remembered the Homecoming party she'd intruded upon. It must be for Deacon, and it made total sense that his entire family would be there.

"Come on, if you're not too tired, I'll give you a tour. You can meet everyone later when it's not such an overwhelming crowd," Piper offered.

"I'd like that. Thank you, Piper." Amaira breathed a sigh of relief and gratefully followed Piper out the front door and as far away from Deacon as she could possibly get without causing a bigger scene.

<hr>

Deacon ignored the throbbing in his side as he watched Amaira walk away, her hips swaying tantalizingly, and her silky black hair tumbling down to her waist. His fingers itched to have those strands wrapped around them, and he wondered if it was a soft as it looked. A cough from somewhere to his right brought him back to his senses to find his sister watching him with her arms crossed. Amy's cheeks were as bright as her hair, and Deacon swore under his breath.

"What the hell do you think you're doing?" She yelled, silencing what little conversation there was in the room, and dragging every pair of eyes in his direction. "Mom's going to be so pissed if you popped a single stitch!"

"I'm fine, Amy." He lied, grimacing as the throbbing pain intensified.

"Yeah, right. And I'm Tinkerbell, hold on while I go find my fairy wings." She ignored the chuckles that followed her comment and stormed over to Deacon's side. "You promised not to overexert yourself, Deeks."

Seeing the concern in her hazel eyes, Deacon sighed and let her lead him to an armchair in the corner. He grimaced as she fussed over him, hating all the attention but recognizing his sister's need to reassure herself. He knew she was terrified of loosing him again, ignoring the stab of guilt that seared through his gut. Deacon placed a hand on Amy's arm, and she paused in her ministrations to make him more comfortable, looking up at him questioningly.

"I'm sorry I scared you, kiddo." He quietly apologized. "I'll try to be more careful. You don't need to worry. I'm not going anywhere, I promise."

Amy nodded, dashing her tears away on her sleeve and refusing to look at him. She stood and threw her arms around him, squeezing him tightly and burying her head in his shoulder.

Chapter 4

*"One night I caught Rose sneaking into the barn. It was then I
discovered she'd been sleeping in it since her parents had kicked
her out. She had nowhere else to go and feared I would tell my
parents and get her fired before she could save enough to get her
own place. She was too afraid of people judging her if they knew,
so she kept it to herself this whole time. It took some convincing,
but I finally convinced her to talk to my parents. They instantly
took her in and stuck me in the same room with Trent. It sucked
sharing a room with my brother, but something changed between
Rose and I after that." -Travis's journal*

Amaira nearly twisted her ankle when her heel got stuck in a
patch of uneven ground. She swore and slipped her foot out of the
shoe, bending down to yank on it as the grass tickled her toes.
This was the last thing she needed right now, but she refused to
leave Xander's family with the impression that she was a lunatic
or something, so she tamped down the desire to explode and
yanked on the shoe mercilessly until the earth opened around it
and sent her flying backwards.

"Oomph!" She yelped as her backside hit the cold, hard
ground, knocking the air out of her. She looked up to see that
Piper had paused and turned back in time to see her gracelessly
sprawling in the dirt. Piper chuckled and headed back to lend her
a helping hand.

"Sorry about that. I guess I should have warned you that you
might want to think about wearing sneakers or boots while you're
staying here. Farm life, even in an orchard, is killer on heels,"
Piper explained as Amaira regained her balance and slipped the
cursed heel back on her foot. "Are you alright?"

"Yeah, nothing more than a bruised ego and sore behind. Please don't offer me anything hard to sit on for awhile and I might be able to sit later without embarrassing myself further," Amaira muttered, dusting the dirt off her pants.

"I'll try to keep that in mind," Piper replied with a laugh. "Come on. Last I saw Xander, he was over by the plum trees."

"Plum trees?" Amaira found herself asking. "I thought this was an apple orchard."

"Mmmhmm. We used to be, but in the past decade or so we've expanded our produce to include plums, pears, cherries, and various kinds of berries grow over behind the new barn on the far side of the farm. Follow this path here," she pointed to a dirt path worn in the grass that led around behind what Amaira assumed must be the old barn, and disappeared behind it, "and it will take you there. It also leads to my home, so if you ever need anything or Deacon's getting out of hand or you simply need someone to talk to, come on over. I'm usually pretty easy to find."

"Thank you," Amaira's frustration quickly gave way to a warming sensation in her belly. She liked Deacon's stepmother. Piper was kind and welcoming, unlike the man himself. Amaira opened her mouth to ask why she lived so close by, when a flash of red caught her eye and she turned towards it. Xander stood talking to a giant bear of a man with a short and tidy beard and greying blond hair. Even from this distance she could see the striking resemblance between him and Deacon. A few feet beyond them, a woman stood staring out at the trees. She was dressed in a conservative black dress, her arms wrapped around herself, for warmth or comfort Amaira couldn't tell, but it was her hair that had caught Amaira's eye. Twisted back into a simple bun, she easily recognized the woman by her dark red hair. The woman so many of Xander's fans had wondered and gossiped about for years. Sarah Hawkins, his wife.

Amaira took a deep breath to calm her racing heart as they approached the trio. She'd been anxious about this trip for weeks, but now that she was face-to-face with the woman, she'd proposed to write a movie about, Amaira found herself wishing she could turn back time and stop herself from blurting out the first idea that came to her mind. Sarah's head turned towards them, and her gaze locked directly on Amaira, coldly examining her before turning back to stare at the trees. Xander nodded in greeting and left Piper to make the introductions as he moved to stand with his wife and wrapped his arms around her. Amaira could hear him whispering softly, but his tone was so low that she couldn't make out what he was saying. Witnessing the intimacy of this moment between them, she realized how out of place she was. She didn't belong here.

"I'm so getting fired," she muttered, tearing her gaze away. The sound of shuffling feet reminded Amaira that she wasn't alone, and she fought the urge to run away and hide in the trees until her audience left. Instead, she plastered a smiled on her face and turned, her hand already out to greet the man that had joined them.

"I'm Jack," he introduced himself, grasping her hand in his rough one and shaking it with a gentility she didn't believe, until that moment, that a man his size could possess. There wasn't a sign of pity or acknowledgement in his expression that told her he'd overheard her, and she was grateful for it.

"Nice to meet you, Jack. I'm Amaira Devan, one of the writers with Film Hawk Productions."

"Welcome to the farm," he replied, his eyes crinkling as he smiled faintly. "You'll have to excuse the cold greeting. It's a sad time for everyone here. I guess Alex forgot about your visit.

You're welcome to stay of course, and if there's anything Piper or I can help you with, please don't hesitate to ask."

"Thank you, that's very kind," Amaira replied with a frown. "I don't understand though, what sad time? I thought it would be a joyous occasion to have your son back?"

"It is. We're all extremely grateful he's returned to us intact. Unfortunately, not everyone we loved could be here to rejoice in the occasion. We just buried Sarah's father, Travis, this morning."

All the blood fled Amaira's body. She was boneless and devasted by her intrusion on this grieving family. Everything clicked into place now, and she realized that it wasn't a home-coming party that she'd inadvertently crashed. It was a wake. Deacon hadn't been deliberately ignoring his guests stares because he was being an inconsiderate buffoon. He simply hadn't wanted to advertise her sudden appearance in a grieving household to friends and family that might take her intrusion as a personal affront on their sorrow. As she stared into the eyes of his father with mixed emotion, she realized she owed Deacon an apology.

"Are you alright?" Jack asked, the corners of his eyes crinkling in concern.

"Oh, yes. I'm fine. I'm a little shocked and very sorry for your loss. I shouldn't be here at all. You should be grieving in privacy. I had no idea. Is there a hotel or something nearby? I passed a bed and breakfast on my way, perhaps they have a room available. I should gather my things and give you all some space." She replied, shivering as a cold breeze blew through the thin fabric of her silk blouse.

"Nonsense. You wanted to write our story, this is part of it," a quiet, feminine voice had Amaira turning to find a graceful, redhaired woman standing a few feet behind her.

29

"Mrs. Hawkins, I'm sorry to be intruding like this. I had no idea your family was grieving," Amaira started to apologize but the other woman waved her off.

"It's all a part of life, unfortunately. My husband would try to protect me from every little painful thing if he could," she smiled sadly. "He also promises that if I do not like the script you come up with, he will toss the entire project. I know how much his production company needs this to be a success though, so I will try my best to be fair in my assessment of your work, Miss..."

"Amaira," she replied automatically, relief warring with her dismay at this woman's revelations. She hadn't realized how much would be riding on her shoulders, but it made sense since the production company was still new and had yet to build a reputation.

"Amaira, please call me Sarah. I imagine we'll be spending a lot of time together while you're here, but if there's anything you need, please don't hesitate to ask anyone here. I hope you don't mind, but I took the liberty of preparing the guestroom for you. I thought you might prefer to be here on the farm instead of alone at a hotel. You could stay in Riley's room while he's away visiting his grandmother for a soccer camp, but I doubt you'd enjoy sleeping in a teenage boy's room. Of course, you'd be here alone with my other son, Deacon. He inherited the farm. If that makes you uncomfortable at all, please let me know. I can try to make alternate arrangements for you," the other woman stated, gesturing towards the house.

"Well actually, Deacon's already offered to sleep in the barn," Amaira answered quietly, and for the first time since she'd joined them, his parents broke into smiles and laughter. Everyone except Sarah, who's frown only deepened.

"He really does take after Travis," Jack joked with a grin. "But I guess he's slept in worse places."

30

"He probably has," Sarah agreed with jerky nod. "But he shouldn't be sleeping anywhere but his own bed in his condition. Especially after signing out of the hospital against medical advice two days ago...."

"Deacon's a grown man, Sarah. He can make his own choices, but I'll keep a close eye on him," Jack promised, sobering.

"Come on," Piper gestured for Amaira to follow her. "I'll show you the rest of this part of the farm."

Amaira was grateful for the escape from the suddenly awkward conversation, but she couldn't help the curiosity that surged through her. Deacon hadn't appeared to be anything but a strong, healthy man when he'd carried her bags inside the house. What could have possibly caused him to end up in the hospital? Did it have anything to do with the sudden homecoming he'd mentioned? She wanted to ask Piper the hundreds of questions that she itched to ask but kept her mouth firmly closed. Instead, she followed Piper towards the small building she'd noticed next to the barn, which turned out to be the market as she'd expected. Though it was closed for obvious reasons, it was filled with wonderfully crafted soaps, and candles and local artwork as well as bins meant for produce and displays for baked goods. Boxes of goods filled the small storage room in the back, making it clear they were in the process of readying it for opening as soon as the season allowed. Which would be soon, she surmised as she followed Piper around, listening to her tour with half an ear. How long does it take to grow stuff anyway? Does it take as long as a man would to recover from injuries received in battle?

Deacon's health was none of her business, she reminded herself. She couldn't help the pangs of guilt that accompanied the idea of him sleeping in the barn if he was ill and prayed, he didn't get worse. She really wished he'd let her leave to find her own lodgings but agreed with his mother that being on the farm might be crucial to her writing. She was stuck between a rock and a hard place… or in this case an extremely hard body.

Chapter 5

"I finally worked up the courage to ask Rose on a date, and immediately after she said yes, my father came in and told us it was going to be a long, cold night in the orchard. There was a late frost threatening our harvest. He divided us up into teams, and Rose volunteered to team up with me. What should have been a horrible, cold, wet night turned out to be the most incredible night of my life. We turned on the hoses and got to work lowering the temperature in the orchard to below freezing to protect the blossoms on the trees from the frost, so they'd still bear fruit. I'd never noticed before how beautiful it all was, seeing the trees and blossoms encased in ice, as if they were part of a crystal palace or something. Rose set up our flashlights in a circle and when I asked what she was doing, she simply replied that she wanted to remember her first date with me by dancing in the moonlight." - *Travis's journal*

The next morning, Amaira stared at the blank screen in frustration. She was convinced the blinking cursor was mocking her. Why couldn't she figure out something to write? An idea, a plan, a word even.... Try as she might, nothing came to mind and she slammed her laptop closed in frustration, groaning as her head landed on top of it.

"Is something wrong?" Deacon asked warily, taking in the sight of Amaira in her rumpled sweats and her hair tossed up in a bun on the top of her head.

"Only everything!" Amaira replied irritably. "How am I ever going to write an epic country romance? I love the city. New York, London, Los Angeles, Paris... those are romantic and exciting places to me. Farms? I don't mean to be rude, but I'm finding it rather hard to believe that anything about farm life could be considered romantic."

Deacon sat in the armchair next to her, stretching his long body out before him as he stared pensively at the wall above her head. He was completely silent, as he sipped his steaming mug of coffee. Amaira chewed her lip, worried that she had insulted him and opened her mouth to apologize. Her apology died on her lips, however, when Deacon shook his head and turned his attention back to her, his eyes boring into her. A shiver traveled up her spine from his sudden attention. She refused to examine it too closely, reminding herself that he was her boss's son. Whatever attraction she was feeling was pointless, he was completely off limits to her.

"There's going to be a late spring frost tonight," he answered cryptically when he finally broke the tense silence between them.

"Frost?" Amaira drew her brows together, desperately wracking her brain for any idea as to what he was talking about and how it might have anything to do with her predicament. "I'm sorry but what does frost have to do with my script? It's going to be cold. So what? Is the furnace broken?"

Deacon chuckled and shook his head.

"No. The furnace is fine. But if you're looking for inspiration, you might want to consider a walk amongst the trees tonight. Dress warmly though. Wouldn't want Jack Frost to bite you too." He grinned, and Amaira fought to contain the butterflies that erupted in her belly at the sight. He rose from his chair before she could ask any more questions and sauntered out of the room, leaving her staring at the doorway he disappeared through.

Frost? She wondered what frost would have to do with making a farm romantic. It was pretty in the winter sometimes, unless of course she was running late and had to scrape it from her car window. Then it was a nuisance, but thankfully she only had to put up with that during the occasional visit to New York when she visited her mother's side of the family. She sighed and slumped in her chair, resolving to dress warmly. It was going to be a chilly night in the orchard apparently. Especially if Deacon was going to force her to stumble through it in the dark to uncover the mystery of his cryptic words.

Chapter 6

"After our first date, everything seemed to happen really fast. Before I knew it, it was our wedding day. We had a small ceremony in the orchard. Just us, our friends and family, and the stars above us to witness our union. I couldn't have asked for a better night." -Travis's journal

Deacon was exhausted. Late spring frosts were his least favourite battle to fight, but if he didn't it could ruin his crops for an entire year. He pulled the tractor to a stop at the main sprinkler shut-off and double checked that it hadn't sprung any leaks. It was freezing out here, and he was soaked after making a quick repair at his last stop. Yanking off his leather gloves, he double checked his watch. It was a few minutes after midnight. Amaira probably wasn't coming if she hadn't made an appearance by now.

Deacon sighed. He didn't blame her for wanting to stay inside where it was warm. She was probably curled up in bed already, all snug and warm under her blankets. His imagination strayed to images of her wearing sexy lingerie, as she laid in wait for him in his bed. He was practically drooling when a snap of a twig caught his attention. He shook his head to snap himself out of his lurid thoughts and blinked, raising an arm to protect his eyes, as the blinding light from a flashlight scorched his eyeballs. After his initial shock wore off, he couldn't help but grin like an idiot.

"It's freezing out here, Deacon! This had better be worth it, or I SWEAR-." Amaira began.

"Trust me. I think you'll like it." Deacon replied, quickly cutting her off.

"Said every man who ever tried to talk a girl into riding him bareback and lived to regret it." She muttered, startling a chuckle out of him. He liked her spunk. "Why are the sprinklers on when it's so cold? The middle of the night seems an odd time to be watering trees."

"Actually, it's the perfect time if I want to protect what blossoms I have on them. The water combined with the cold temperature is covering the entire orchard in ice. It acts like a shield against the frost by lowering the temperature past the frost line and creating a barrier against it. It works to preserve the flowers that would be damaged by the frost. Flowers that will turn into fruit later in the season." Deacon paused, tossing his gloves on the seat of his tractor, before turning back to Amaira.

"But this isn't what I wanted to show you. Come on," he held out his hand, waiting for her to take it. She hesitated a moment, before carefully placing her hand in his. Deacon winked at her and turned to lead her through the dark orchard, their path lit only by the beam of her flashlight. He led her past several rows of trees until they reached a small clearing.

"Wait here," he instructed, leaving her in the middle of the clearing with nothing but her flashlight.

"Can we hurry this up? It's freezing out here!" She called out to him.

"Patience please, it'll be worth the wait." He replied with a soft chuckle, moving through the darkened trees to plug in the strings of lights he had strung up earlier in the evening. His plan was to try and recreate one of his grandfather's journal entries and he prayed that it worked.

Amaira shivered, cursing her idiocy for agreeing to this whole thing. It was freezing out here and she'd almost gotten completely soaked before she realized the sprinklers were on. Not to mention slipping on that patch of ice she hadn't seen in the pitch-black of the night. If anything, she was even more convinced that this whole farm/romance script idea was a total wash. Why had she opened her mouth?

"I'm such a bloody idiot. What am I doing out here anyway? Alone in the dark, in a foreign country, freezing my ass off, and for what? A chance to write a romantic movie script inspired by one of my teenage crushes…. This is nuts." She muttered to herself as she wrapped her arms around her body in a feeble attempt to fend off the cold. Where did Deacon go anyway? Was this a practical joke? Lure the writer into a dark orchard and leave her there to slowly freeze to death?

Amaira opened her mouth to call out to Deacon, deciding to return to the farmhouse if he didn't answer when suddenly the orchard lit up. Strings of delicate lights strung throughout the trees glistened on ice covered leaves and blossoms, making them appear as if they were encased in tiny crystals. She slowly turned in circles, taking it all in. It was breathtakingly beautiful.

"Would you like to dance?"

Startled, Amaira spun around to find Deacon standing behind her, that charming grin she secretly loved spreading across his face.

"There's no music," she whispered, in awe of him and their surroundings. She stared dumbly at his offered hand.

"We'll make our own music," he answered. "Dance with me."

She placed her hand in his and shivered from the contact of his strong, calloused hands. Nodding, she followed as Deacon lead her into a waltz, humming a few bars to a song she didn't recognize. His voice was a deep timbre that sent thrills down her spine and made her heart rate speed up.

"Who sings that?" She asked, desperate to ignore the sensations he was sending through her body. "I can't seem to place the tune."

Deacon looked down into her eyes, their brilliant blue reflecting the golden glow of the delicate lights, pausing as he considered his answer.

"You wont," he replied. "It's from a local band. They haven't played in awhile and weren't very well known when they did play."

"Really? That's too bad. Do you know the lyrics? I'd love to hear some."

"I wouldn't do the song justice," he whispered softly, his warm breath teasing her ear.

"I heard you sing in the shower last night," she replied teasingly. "I know you can carry a tune."

"I didn't realize I had an audience," he replied, smiling down at her. Amaira's cheeks burned in embarrassment, before realizing that his lips hovered barely an inch away from hers. Their breath mingled tantalizingly, clouding around them in the cold night air that was suddenly charged with tension. Time stood still, the seconds ticking by ever so slowly, when Deacon finally broke the spell between them, lowering his forehead to rest on hers. Amaira refused to admit how disappointed she was, even if it was only to herself. They were simply caught up in the moment, she reminded herself, nothing more.

"I have something for you," he whispered, pulling away to dig inside his jacket and pulling out a leather-bound journal.

"What is it?" She asked, intrigued as she reached for the book. Deacon paused for a moment before handing it to her.

"My grandfather's journal. He started writing in it after my grandmother passed. I doubt he even knew I'd found it, but I've never shown it to anyone else before. My mother likely doesn't even know it exists, and if it's possible, I'd prefer you didn't show it to her. It would only open old wounds," he replied over his shoulder as he headed back into the dark depths of the orchard.

"Why give it to me then?" She shouted at his back.

"To give you some background on my family. I thought it might help with your script. Someone's going to tell our story, whether we like it or not. I'd prefer that someone to get it right." He shouted back before disappearing completely into the darkness and leaving her standing there, alone in this icy orchard and longing for his warm embrace. The cold wind whipped through the material of her sweater, making her shiver from the sudden loss of his body heat as she started her journey back to the house.

⁓

Deacon swore under his breath as he struggled not to limp away. The last thing he wanted was for Amaira, or anyone really, seeing how much pain he was in. Especially after he'd almost kissed her. What had he been thinking? His mother would probably murder him if he seduced one of Alex's employees. But her lips were so full and tempting, it had taken nearly every ounce of willpower to stop himself. A girl like her was likely looking for a real relationship anyway. That was something he couldn't offer her. As much as he'd love to spend a few days or weeks in bed with her, his heart was completely off limits. He'd made that mistake once and refused to repeat it. He'd joined the army and left this place that he loved, because he couldn't bear being here anymore. It was bad enough that his ex-girlfriend had cheated on him and gotten pregnant. The man she claimed she'd cheated with, however... Deacon had left to avoid destroying his family, choosing to keep it a secret and sending her money regularly to keep her quiet. One heartbreak was bad enough. He wouldn't risk his family. He couldn't.

Amaira, however, now she was a different kind of woman. If he let it happen, she could have the power to wreak all kinds of havoc on his heart. The last thing he wanted though, was for that havoc to drive him away from his home again. No, he decided, Amaira was not for him. There were plenty of women he could have a roll in the haystack with, that would do far less damage.

Safe in the darkness of the orchard once again, he turned and watched as Amaira headed towards the house, the light from her flashlight skipping ahead of her. Once she was out of sight, he forced his thoughts from her full lips and gently swaying hips and hauled himself up into the tractor to make one last pass through the orchard to inspect the sprinklers again before his dad took over for the rest of the night.

Chapter 7

"It was Rose that wanted to stay on the farm with my family. I wanted us to get a place of our own so we could be alone, but she wanted nothing to do with it. She loved the farmhouse with all its creaking floorboards and rattling pipes." -Travis's journal.

The next night, Amaira puttered around the kitchen, bored out of her mind. It was late, and she should probably be sleeping, but she couldn't help the restlessness that surged through her. She wished she could have been home to see her father get his award tonight. As it was, Hamir had filmed the entire thing and sent it to her. She ignored his offer to explain anything they discussed that she didn't understand. Some scientists could be quite pretentious around other people but spending her entire youth in a home with two scientists had prepared her for that eventuality. Being excluded from their conversations around the dinner table simply because she didn't understand what they were discussing no longer bothered her the way it had when she was younger. She imagined it was the same for them when she and her mother discussed fashion or sugar plum fairies.

On top of missing home and her family, the farmhouse was creepy at night. It was darker than she was used to, and the sounds of the house settling had her imagination on overtime. It was the perfect setting for a thriller script. There was no one around for miles and miles. It would be so easy for someone to come in here and murder her in the middle of the night. The creaking floorboards and rickety pipes could easily be masking the sounds of a stalker's footsteps. Even the shadows seemed to loom over her, dark and sinister as if they held a dark secret. She shivered and tried to shake it off, opening a pantry door in search of a late-night snack.

A few minutes later, with a bowl of popcorn in hand, she sauntered into the living room and settled in on the big comfy couch. She turned the television on and started flicking through the channels before settling on a movie. She'd watched Harry Potter a hundred times at least, but it was still one of her favourites.

Halfway through the movie, she heard a definite click of a door closing and footsteps slowly coming closer. She screamed and jumped off the couch, dashing through the entryway and colliding with a rather large man. Amaira shrieked again and instinctively struck out at her attacker, letting years of self defense training take over as she struggled to get away. The man grunted when she landed a particularly well-placed strike to his solar plexus, but he still managed to hold on to her. He wrapped his arms tightly around her body, pinning her arms to her sides as she struggled against him.

"Amaira!" He shouted, but she didn't stop to wonder how the intruder knew her name. Fear coursed through her body, triggering her fight or flight instincts. "Amaira, stop! It's me, Deacon! I'm not going to hurt you."

He held her tight, repeating his mantra that he wouldn't hurt her, until she'd settled enough to hear him. When it was clear she wouldn't keep fighting him, he let her go and took several cautious steps back, glancing into the living room behind her.

"What were you watching?" He asked curiously. "Is that Harry Potter? Did you think I was a Dementor or something? I mean, I've never really thought of Harry Potter as being a scary movie, but I guess it could be to someone...."

"It's not," Amaira answered shakily, embarrassed by her outburst and still a bit skittish. "I freaked myself out being alone in this strange house in the middle of nowhere. I put the movie on

43

hoping it would help me relax. Harry Potter and the Prisoner of Azkhaban is one of my favourites."

"I'm sorry if I freaked you out. I never meant to scare you. I was going to grab a hot shower and some fresh clothes for the morning before heading back out to the barn for the night. I didn't realize you were still awake, or I would have announced myself when I came in," Deacon apologized, absently rubbing the spot where she'd struck him.

"It's... it's alright," she replied. "I was already pretty wound up before you came in. I'm sorry I freaked out. My imagination got the best of me tonight."

"Well, if you're alright, I guess I'll go grab my stuff and head out," he started up the stairs, but Amaira couldn't bear the idea of being alone in the house after that fright. A pang of guilt ate at her as she remembered that the only reason, he was sleeping in the barn was to make her more comfortable here to begin with. She'd essentially kicked him out of his own home.

"Wait," she called out. "Y-you don't have to sleep in the barn. It must be pretty cold out there at night."

Deacon stared at her for a moment, assessing the situation. He glanced from her to the living room and back again before opening his mouth and closing it again. He nodded and all the anxiety she'd been consumed with for the past couple hours instantly fled. Deacon didn't say a word as he came back down the stairs and followed her into the living room to settle in an ancient armchair across from where she resumed her spot on the sofa.

"Any popcorn left?" He asked, and Amaira handed him the bowl, grateful for both his presence and the lack of judgement. "So, I have one question. Are you a Hufflepuff or a Ravenclaw?"

"How do you know I'm not a Slytherin or Gryffindor?" She asked indignantly, sitting opposite him, and crossing her legs. She noticed that his gaze dropped with the movement, following her legs, and she could barely suppress a grin. She was tempted to do it again.

"Not devious enough for a Slytherin," he responded, then shrugged. "I guess you could be a Gryffindor. You've got a mean right hook."

"I don't even need to guess what you are," she replied. "Gryffindor is practically written all over your face."

Deacon grinned and popped a kernel into his mouth. A scream dragged their attention back to the screen and they settled in to watch the rest of the movie. The next hour was spent munching on popcorn and discussing their favourite films from their childhoods. Amaira stretched and yawned, surprised to discover the movie had long since finished. She couldn't remember a time when she'd had that much fun talking so late at night. Life after college had become so consumed with pursuing her dreams and making rent, that she hadn't realized how lonely she'd become. It had been nearly two years since she'd had any kind of relationship... or even a date she realized.

Deacon reached over and hit the power button on the remote to turn off the television. Stretching, he stood and offered a hand to Amaira. Helping her off the couch, they climbed the stairs and said goodnight at the top. Amaira paused outside her bedroom door, watching Deacon's back as he headed for the shower to wash off the day's dirt and grime. She barely contained a sigh as the door clicked behind him. She quickly stepped into her room and shut the door before sinking onto her bed with a sigh. Nothing good could possibly come from lusting after Deacon Mackenzie. She had to nip this crush of hers in the bud before the cost became her dream career as a screenwriter. Watching his ass move in those tight jeans of his though... now that wouldn't be a career ending crime, right? Exhausted, Amaira collapsed on the bed and shut her eyes. It wasn't long before sleep claimed her, her earlier fears forgotten as she sank into a restless slumber.

Dreaming of Deacon

Chapter 8

"There are so many memories that I have labelled in the past as the best time of my life, and yet something new always seems to surpass that. I doubt anything could have beaten the night our daughter was born. The first time I held Sarah my heart was so full it was near to exploding... and she screamed like a banshee! The little bit of hair on her head was already gleaming with hints of red. Rose joked that it was all the Irish in her, but I think it's the Mackenzie spirit that's got it's hook in her." -Travis's journal

Amaira woke to the sound of shuffling feet, and whispers. They sounded as if they were right next to her bed, and she kept her eyes closed and listened, tensing in fear beneath her blankets. She had no idea who was in her room, or why, but she didn't want to give away her advantage of surprise until she knew for sure what was happening.

"She's so pretty, don't you think so Amy?" The youthfulness of the feminine voice surprised her, and the pit of fear in her stomach slowly began to dissipate.

"Sure, if you like that Hollywood glamour," another voice whispered from across the room. "We really shouldn't be in here, Tana. Let's wait downstairs for her."

"Deacon seems to think she's pretty," the girl named Tana sighed. "I saw them dancing in the orchard last night when I was helping my dad take over sprinkler duty. It was so romantic."

"Deacon's not exactly a great judge of character. Remember Layla? Can we please get out of here before she wakes up? This is seriously creepy Tana." The first girl, Amy, pointed out.

"Yes, it is very creepy," Amaira agreed, rolling over to find a slender, red-headed teenager standing inside the doorway and a shorter blond that reminded her of Deacon's stepmother, Piper, near the dresser on the far side of the room. "I must look like Medusa with all of this bedhead."

"I am so sorry! We didn't mean to wake you. We only came up to see if you wanted to join us for some yoga out by the lake. It's nearly nine, and we thought you would be awake," the redheaded girl flushed, her arms crossing protectively in front of her body as she apologized.

"Yoga by the lake sounds wonderful," Amaira smiled sympathetically, hoping to put the girl at ease. "I didn't realize I'd slept so late. Why don't you wait for me downstairs and I'll get ready?"

"See Amy. I told you she had to be nice if your dad let her come here! I'm Tana," the shorter blond girl introduced herself with a giant grin and made no move to leave. "We're Deacon's half-sisters."

"Tana? I'd like to say it's lovely to meet you, but I would much rather become acquainted with you both after I've had a chance to wake up and smell the coffee," Amaira yawned and stretched.

Tana practically leaped away from the dresser in her rush towards the door that Amy had already vanished through.

"Of course. I'll go put a pot on for you while we wait. Deacon will probably want some too," she replied, following Amy out the door and shutting it quietly behind her.

Once the girls were gone, Amaira rolled over and pulled the covers back over her head with a groan, hoping to fall back asleep for another hour, but it was no use. She was wide awake now. Tossing her blankets off with a huff, she slid out of bed and slowly made her way to the closet, then made a detour to her bedroom door and flicked the lock. She didn't want to take a chance that one of Deacon's precocious sisters invaded her room while she dressed.

Twenty minutes later, dressed in yoga pants and a loose-fitting burgundy sweater that gathered around her waist, Amaira stepped into the hallway. Closing the door behind her, she turned and narrowly avoided crashing into another person.

"Sorry," she apologized, taking in the beautiful, tall, and fair woman standing before her. "I didn't realize anyone else was still up here. Are you another one of Deacon's relatives?"

"Maybe someday if I'm lucky," the woman replied with a sly smile that quickly changed to calculating as she assessed Amaira. "I'm Paris. I come here regularly to... take care of him. And who are you exactly?"

"I'm Amaira. I work with Deacon's stepfather," Amaira introduced herself, ignoring the giant stone that started to form in the pit of her stomach. The way the other woman said the words *take care of him*, left little room for doubt. Clearly last night had meant nothing to Deacon if he could be with another woman a few short hours later. When did he make a booty call? They didn't get to bed until quite late, and it was still early in the morning. Early enough for his sisters be here at least. Did they know about her? If they did, she supposed they wouldn't have made those comments about Deacon being interested in her. But they had mentioned his poor choices in the women he dated. Was this one of them?

Or was Amaira the other woman? Nausea roiled through her at the thought, and she shook her head to clear her muddled brain. She was a guest here, an employee. Deacon was her boss's stepson. She had no claims to him, and no right to expect anything from him, she reminded herself. This woman standing before her was clearly familiar with him and this house, she realized as she watched as Paris sauntered down the hall to his room with a sly grin on her face.

"It was nice meeting you," she called over her shoulder as she opened the door to his room and stepped inside without a moment's hesitation.

"Yeah," Amaira ignored the sudden thickness in her throat as she replied. "Nice to meet you too."

She didn't know how long she stood there, staring at the closed door. Seconds turned to minutes, which could easily have been hours before one of Deacon's sisters called up to her from the bottom of the stairs. Loud grunts and a crash came from the other side of his bedroom door, spurring Amaira into action as she raced down the stairs, trying to get as far away as she possibly could. Amaira ignored the ache in her heart and the tears that threatened to choke her as she followed Deacon's sisters down to the lake.

~~~~

Deacon groaned and wished he could roll under the covers and hide from the blinding light that flooded his room. He sucked in a sharp breath at the pain that seared through his side, trying not to flinch away from the gentle fingers that teased at his bandages.

"I swear your trying to tear my skin off," he grumbled instead, wincing as the nurse that came to change his bandages pulled off a long strip of tape and shoved it into a garbage bag before tackling the next strip. She glanced up at him from under her lashes and Deacon swore she rolled her eyes at him. Or she was trying to flirt with him. It had been so long since he'd flirted with a woman he couldn't tell anymore.

"I didn't realize big, strong men like you were such babies. How do you keep managing to pop these stitches anyway? You know you shouldn't be doing anything too strenuous in your condition. This shouldn't need bandaging anymore," she muttered.

Deacon grimaced as she worked, her strong fingers deftly removing the last of the bandages and working the gauze off his wound. He grunted when she started prodding the sensitive skin and tried to throw an arm over his eyes, preferring not to look at his disformed body. Instead, he disturbed her small workstation next to the bed, scattering all her tools and knocking the fresh bandages to the floor. The table she was using hit the ground with a crash.

"Damnit Deacon!" She shouted, groaning when she realized the saline had also spilled onto the floor.

"Sorry Paris. Here let me help you with that," he moved to try and get up to help. However, a turtle on its shell struggling to roll over was more graceful than he was in his attempts to sit up on the edge of his bed.

"You stay put," Paris said, quickly picking up the clean bandages from the floor before the saline could spread to them. "I'll clean this up and be right back to finish what I started. You're lucky your cute."

Deacon grinned as he watched her walk out the door. If it wasn't for the exotic beauty who'd intoxicated his senses the moment she'd stepped out of her car, he might be tempted to take Paris up on the invitation that lit her eyes as she left the room. But Amaira... it took every bit of willpower to tear himself away from her and the temptation to taste her lips last night. He had to keep reminding himself that she was an employee of his stepfather's. She was there to work and was strictly off limits. Even if every sway of her hips screamed with sinful promise.

Her first view of the lake took her breath away. She could see all the way to the other side of the lake, with its city skylines in the distance and dotted with sailboats. Amy and Tana headed in the direction of a large weeping willow tree, and she could see a pair of mats already set up beneath its branches. Amaira quickly followed behind and set up her yoga mat beside them, facing out towards the peaceful lake.

"It's about time you ladies showed up," Piper called out as she and Sarah jogged towards them from the rocky shore.

"Someone was sleeping in," Tana answered with a nod in Amaira's direction.

"Deacon had me out in the orchards late the other night," Amaira replied, flushing under his mother's scrutinizing gaze. "He was teaching me about his technique to protect the crops from frost. And I've been having trouble sleeping in a new place, getting used to all the sounds of the house settling at night has my imagination on overdrive."

"Oh, I also let Paris in," Amy informed her mother as she started to stretch. "Deacon probably won't be too happy about it though."

"He should have thought about that before leaving the hospital and throwing himself back into farming so soon," Sarah replied. "Now, let's start with the Mountain Pose."

52

Amaira followed them through the various poses, enjoying the wonderful stretch in the fresh air. She wondered about Deacon's injury, having heard it mentioned before, and decided she might need to ask his sisters about it. She hoped he would tell her first, however, since she hated the idea of prying into his private life. He didn't act like an injured or sick man would. At least, not like any she was familiar with.

As soon as they were finished with their cool down stretches, Amaira plopped down on her mat, cross legged, and jotted down a few quick notes in her notebook. Mostly rambling thoughts, intertwined with descriptions of the scene around her. She was lost in thought for several moments, and nearly missed Tana and Piper sidling up next to her, the elder loudly clearing her throat to gain her attention.

"Sorry! Did you say something? I tend to get caught up in the moment when inspiration strikes," Amaira apologized with a start.

"It's alright, I get the same way with a camera in my hands. I was only asking if anyone wanted to go for a swim in the lake to cool down," Piper shrugged.

"A swim in the lake… in May? Isn't it a bit chilly for that?" Amaira gaped. There was no way she was swimming in a lake at this time of year.

"She's kidding," Tana laughed. "Come on, I'll walk you back to the house so you can keep writing whatever it is that you're writing. Unless you want to get caught in the rain?"

"Rain?" Amaira glanced up at the sky. She hadn't noticed any rain clouds during their workout but realized that Tana was right. A storm was blowing in quickly judging by the dark clouds overhead and the wind picking up speed. "It does get pretty hard to write on wet paper."

Tana and Piper chuckled and helped her stand and gather her things. With their mats rolled, they followed Amy and Sarah back to the farmhouse, chatting until they all parted paths near the barn. Piper and Tana took the dirt path that Piper had pointed out the day she'd arrived, jogging as the first drops of rain began to fall. Sarah and Amy loaded their mats and bags into the back of a silver Lexus SUV and climbed in, waving to her as they backed out of their parking spot. Thunder clapped, startling Amaira, and with her notebook clutched to her chest and the strap of her mat slung over her shoulder, she raced inside.

Chapter 9

"The loss of our second child... I don't know what to say about that. It broke Rose and I, and I have no idea how to make anything better. I had no idea how to ease my own pain... I can't imagine the depths of hers." -Travis's journal

The storm raged outside as Amaira stared at the leatherbound journal taunting her from where it laid on the table next to her coffee. She'd jotted down everything she could think of already, but nothing solid enough to begin her script with so far. Deacon was probably upstairs still with his "nurse" or waiting out the storm in the barn. She hadn't seen him all morning, and with the storm picking up speed outside she doubted she would be seeing anyone soon that could help her with her research.

"So, how's the movie or whatever, coming along?" Jack casually strode into the kitchen, making a beeline for the fresh pot of coffee she'd made a few minutes ago, startling her with his sudden appearance.

"It could be going a lot better," she admitted sheepishly, after her heart rate returned to a normal pace. "I have nowhere to start since I'm not allowed to use the Mexico debacle in the script. And I really don't wish to bother the Hawkins while they're grieving. I know they said I could stay and write the script, but it doesn't feel right. I'm intruding on their privacy and that's not what I intended when I blurted out this idea."

"I get it," Jack poured himself a steaming mug and eased himself into a chair across from her at the scarred kitchen table. "Those two have always been in their own little world. It's hard being the one on the outside looking in sometimes. I don't have all the details, but I might be of some help for you. After all, I

55

probably know Sarah better than anyone since we grew up together. My story and hers are intertwined."

"I'd hate to tear you away from work, but I would be so grateful for any help you can give me." Amaira leaned forward, eagerly flipping open her notebook to a fresh page and clicking her pen.

"Is it strange, working on the farm where your ex-wife grew up?" She asked.

"Not at all," Jack smiled. "But Sarah and I were never married. We grew up together. Sarah's my best friend, my first love, and the mother of my first born. We fought a lot in our senior year of high school, and in retaliation, she started dating this jerk from the rugby team. I hated him and I was also terrified of the feelings I had for her. So, I did what any logical teenage boy would do. I kissed another girl and pushed her away. Right into the arms of the biggest bully in our school, but she was willfully blind to his faults. Anyway, after we graduated, he proposed to her, and they started planning a life together. It nearly broke my heart, and I decided to go away to college. Except when it came time to leave, I couldn't without telling her the truth about how I felt. Even if she didn't feel the same way, at least I wouldn't have any regrets. Turned out she did share my feelings and we ended up making love for the first time that night. Neither of realized at the time that it would be the only time we ever made love. In the morning, I climbed onboard an airplane and made my way to New York. She was supposed to break things off with the other guy, while I worked on transferring to a school closer to home," Jack paused, staring out the window and sipping absent-mindedly from his mug.

"My mother had other plans, however, and told Sarah that I wanted nothing to do with her, and I was never leaving New York. Sarah believed her and instead of waiting for me like she promised, she eloped with my high school bully. I was heartbroken when I'd learned about it, and at the time, I had no idea of my mother's involvement. One day, her husband showed up on campus and tracked me down somehow. He confronted me about sleeping with his wife. I tried to deny it because I didn't want to make her life more complicated. I was worried about what he might do if he knew. Except he wouldn't let me deny it. That's when I found out about Sarah's pregnancy. Her husband was furious, and I didn't understand why he didn't believe he could be the father. After all, we'd only made love the one time. I thought he was trying to get out of his responsibilities as a man and a husband and a soon to be father and I called him out on it. Instead of getting righteous or throwing a fist at me like I expected, he broke down. I've never seen a man look more defeated than he did in that moment.

Apparently, he had gotten an injury playing rugby when he was younger, that prevented him from being able to have children. That's how he knew Sarah's child had to be mine. Until senior year, everyone had thought she and I would be together forever because we were always glued to each other's side. There hadn't been anyone else for either of us. But I was so hurt by her betrayal that I couldn't see past it. I'm ashamed to admit that I wasn't the man I should have been in that moment, and as time went on, it became harder to fix my mistakes. Her ex-husband raised Deacon as his own until he was twelve, but he made Sarah's life a complete hell. He cheated on her regularly, and verbally abused her. To this day, she's never shared with me how toxic their marriage became. But from what I saw after their divorce, it was bad.

She caught him in the act one day, and kicked him out, but it took a toll on her. She was depressed for a long time. By then I had come to terms with our past, and I returned to the farm to try and be a father and repair whatever I could of our relationship. I couldn't spring myself on her after she had suffered such a devastating blow, so I waited on the sidelines. I missed my chance of reconnecting with her romantically, but it turned out for the better if you ask me. Her friend Angie took her to Mexico to try and help her move past the divorce, and that's when she met Alex… Xander… whatever you want to call him," he paused to take a sip of his coffee while Amaira tried to write all of the information he'd shared down for future reference.

"Dad! There you are! Mom's been looking everywhere for you. She needs help with her gallery pieces and needs "her giant Viking for inspiration." That's seriously gross by the way," Tana stuck a finger down her throat and pretended to gag.

Jack coughed as he choked on his coffee, his eyes practically bugging out of his head as he struggled not to laugh. Startled, Amaira glanced up from her notes to find Tana standing in a doorway that connected the kitchen to the screened-in porch on the back of the house. The storm had blown over while they sat there talking and she hadn't noticed.

"Guess that's my cue," he said with a chuckle, pushing his chair back as he stood and making his way to the sink. He quickly washed his mug and set it on the rack to dry. At the door he turned back to Amaira and nodded at the journal in front of her. "We can talk more later if you like. Whatever that is, why don't you give it a read and see if it'll help in the meantime."

Amaira leaned back on her chair, staring at the cracked leather journal in front of her. The screen door closed behind Jack, and she was left alone with it once again. Why was she resisting the urge to open it? Groaning, she gave up the fight and slid the book towards her, opening it carefully as she turned the fragile pages.

October 19th

I feel ridiculous, but I promised my mother that I would try. She's worried about me, and I don't blame her. But this journaling thing… it's not really my style. Still, I did promise and I'm a man of my word. I only hope my baby girl never finds this thing, or else forgives me for lying to her about her mother when she does. It was probably the worst thing I could have done, but I refuse to let her grow up with even the tiniest notion that she's responsible for her mother's death. It's absolutely bull shit of course, but grief can make people think strange things and that's the last thing I want for Sarah. She doesn't need to grow up with that black cloud over her head. It's far better that she thinks her mother wasn't well and abandoned us. It's better that she believes her mother might be out in the world living a happier life, instead of resting beneath her favourite willow tree by the lake.

I'm still not entirely sure what happened that night, but Rose had been unwell for awhile. The toll of several miscarriages had wreaked havoc on her mental health as well as her body, and the last one undid her. I should have seen the warning signs, but I missed every single one of them. The day she took Sarah grocery shopping and forgot Sarah in the car a few weeks ago…. She was so distraught with guilt! I never should have let her get behind the wheel of her car. I told myself she just needed to blow off some steam and she would come right home afterwards. I never imagined that she would drive the station wagon into a tree…. I'll never know if it was accident or if she meant to do it….

Amaira gasped, quickly shutting the book. How tragic for the Mackenzie's to suffer through the loss of a wife and mother. She wanted to cry for them and wondered if Sarah still had no idea where her mother was. She couldn't imagine how hard that must have been for them. She jotted down a few notes in her notebook and packed everything away. The emotional toll in that one passage had her desperate to take a break. That and the growling of her stomach. She grabbed her phone and started googling for Indian Chinese food that delivered out here.

Chapter 10

"Sarah's growing up so fast. I'm in awe of my little girl. I remember the day she started walking. It was her first play date with a little boy named Jackson from a neighbouring farm. He was already walking, and Sarah refused to be left behind, so she got up and trotted across the room like she'd been doing it all along. I said it then and I'll say it again. It's the Mackenzie blood that drives her determination." -Travis's journal

Deacon wiped the sweat from his face and neck with a rag he'd pulled out of his back pocket. He was already missing the cool spring air, as he climbed off the tractor, remembering the night he'd spent dancing with Amaira under the full moon. There was nothing he wanted as much as the chance to hold her in his arms again. She had been cold towards him since the night in the orchard however, so he doubted she would be open to any advances from him. Which was a shame since he really wanted to advance their relationship. Catching sight of a cherry red sportscar parked in front of his grandparents... no, his house he corrected himself... he steeled his spine for a confrontation he should have anticipated. What surprised him most was how long it had taken for her to show up on his doorstep.

Approaching the porch with caution, he shoved his hands in his pockets, resisting the urge to cross them over his chest. Irritation and anger filled him when he spotted her sitting in his grandfathers rocking chair with her long legs crossed and her perfectly manicured fingernails tapping on the wooden arm.

"What brings you to the countryside Layla? If you're looking for fresh produce, I'd be happy to direct you to the market," he didn't even bother trying to be anything more than cordial as he waited on the bottom step for her answer.

"Deacon, sweetheart, you've been gone so long, I thought you might like to see your daughter," she replied with a sickly-sweet smile on her face.

Deacon glanced back at the car, looking for any sign of the little girl Layla had given birth too and left on her parent's doorstep when she realized he wasn't going to play the doting boyfriend, and whisk her away to LA. Assured there was no child in the hot car, he turned back towards his ex-girlfriend, and took a slow perusal of her toned and tanned body clad in a skimpy denim skirt and silk blouse. She arched a brow and tossed her long, golden brown curls over her shoulder.

"I'd be happy to spend some time with your daughter, Layla, but you seem to have forgotten to bring her," he replied refusing, and failing miserably, to let her get under his skin. "Stop bullshitting me. Why are you really here?"

"The army stopped sending your child support checks. I came to find out why. What the hell is going on Deacon?" Layla rose from her perch and moved closer; fury and greed laced her every movement and he wondered how he'd never noticed how truly ugly she was beneath all her fancy clothes and banging body. She was gorgeous and she used it to manipulate men into doing what she wanted. Was that how she snared Alex into her web of lies? He shook his head to clear it. No matter what she said, Alex cheating on his mother still didn't make any sense.

"Why should I keep paying support for a child that isn't mine?" He demanded, his frustration with this situation making his blood boil. It was the entire reason he'd joined the army in the first place. At the time it seemed like the best idea to avoid the impending confrontation, and the harm it would do to his family if the truth ever came out. Now, he didn't give a damn if it did. His brother and sister were old enough to handle it now. Layla could make whatever claims she wanted, as loudly as she wanted too.

"You claimed her as your own, the minute you paid that first support check. Or have you forgotten our deal? Either she's yours, or I tell the world who her father really is. It'll destroy your whole fucking family, Deacon. Is that what you want?" She screeched, taking a threatening step forward.

He would have been amused by her threat of physical violence, but he really didn't care for the drama that would cause on its own. She'd use so much as a broken nail caused by slapping him or catching it on something as evidence that he'd abused her. How he had ever let himself fall for such a she-devil was beyond his grasp. He took in her perfect makeup, and expensive highlights and wondered what he had ever seen in her. The woman had never been interested in anything to do with him, and everything to do with how close he could get her to the famous Xander Hawkins. Right into his bedroom if her claims were true. It would devastate his mother if she ever found out. She'd caught her first husband having sex with his babysitter, and later found out that he'd been cheating on her practically from the moment they'd said, "I do." When he'd agreed to Layla's extortion, he'd hoped to avoid seeing her get hurt again. Only this time it would destroy her, as she's been madly in love with Xander since the day they'd met. It wasn't until he'd come home from the hospital and seen how gentle and caring Xander was around Sarah, that it reminded him of how much she meant to his stepfather. Now he had no doubt that Layla's claims were boldfaced lies meant to hurt him and a pathetic attempt to keep stringing him along.

"You do what you've got to do. If you don't mind, I've got a farm to run," he pushed past her when she refused to move out of his way and reached for the screen door just as Amaira pushed it open.

"I thought I heard voices out here," she said, glancing around and taking in the scene before her. Deacon could only wonder what this must look like to her and shoved a hand through his sweaty hair. "I'm sorry, I didn't mean to interrupt anything."

"Not at all, sweetheart," he said with a smile, hoping she would play along. "The lady was just a little lost. Looking for something that isn't here anymore."

"Deacon?" Layla asked, confusion mixed with condescension lacing her voice. "Who is this and what desert did you dig *her* up in?"

～

Amaira's hackles rose. She was sorry for interrupting them, she had no idea who was outside talking when she'd come to the door, or she never would have stepped outside. Then she wished the Earth would open-up and swallow her whole when she discovered the voices belonged to Deacon and yet another woman. Seriously, the man was gorgeous, but did he really have to sleep with every woman who threw herself at his feet? They were everywhere! Just as she resolved to never join his harem, the other woman opened her mouth and pissed her right off. *What desert did he dig her up in?* Death Valley bitch! Pasting on a smile, Amaira rose on her toes and pressed a lingering kiss to Deacon's mouth, her lips tingling from the brief contact, before turning her attention on the diva wannabe with her matching hot pink lips and nails.

Was it her imagination, or was Deacon grinning when she let out a loud *"Kutiya"*? Did he understand what she was saying? He probably wouldn't thank her for calling one of his girlfriends a bitch, but she was beyond caring. The ignorant witch needed to be put in her place. Amaira wished she could condescend enough to drag her behind the barn by her hair and shove her in the compost heap, but her parents raised her to be better. She pulled herself up to her full height, tossed her hair over her shoulder and smiled up at Deacon adoringly, ignoring the other woman completely.

"Deacon, sweetheart, you neglected to mention that we were expecting company," Amaira mimicked her grandmother's accent as best she could and continued to mutter insults in Hindi under her breath. He wrapped a strong arm around her waist and pulled her to his side, nuzzling her hair as his fingers lazily stroked her hip, weakening her resolve to never join his harem. She doubted she'd say no if he pulled her inside and made love to her in front of the fireplace. Amaira blinked a couple times, desperately trying to reel in her imagination before it got the better of her.

"Amaira, my love, this is Layla. The ex-girlfriend I told you about," he leaned in closer to her and loudly whispered in her ear, "the crazy one I flew into a war zone to avoid."

"Oh yes! I'm so glad I have a chance to finally thank you. If it weren't for you, Deacon and I would never have met," Amaira smiled serenely. "Please, you must stay for dinner. I ordered plenty Indian Chinese food. You can tell me all about how you drove Deacon away."

"Ugh, no. I don't eat cats." Layla tossed her hair over her shoulder, her arms crossed over her chest as she tapped her foot on the wooden porch, clearly getting angrier by the minute.

"Cats? Deacon, dear, do you eat cats? Strange customs you have here. *Ghinauna!* I'm so glad you're a vegetarian now," Amaira stuck a finger down her throat and mimed how disgusting she found the idea of eating cats. Deacon snorted with amusement.

"Whatever. You'll be hearing from my lawyers by the end of the week, Deacon," Layla turned on her heel and stomped towards a red car parked inches away from the first step. She climbed in and slammed the door before turning the car around and screeching down the driveway, kicking up a cloud of dust in her wake.

"What the hell was that all about, *Sweetheart,*" Amaira asked when they were finally alone.

Deacon blew out a long breath, releasing her to pinch the bridge of his nose. His eyes squeezed tightly shut for a few moments.

"It's a long story," he replied quietly, "but I'd rather not share it here. Come on, let's go for a ride and get out of here for a bit."

He tilted his head towards his shiny black truck. Amaira stared at him for a moment, fighting the urge to stay where she was and remain blissfully ignorant of his past relationships. She took another glance at his strained expression and caved to her need to know more about this man and headed to his truck.

Chapter 11

"We really thought this pregnancy would the one. Sarah was going to have a little brother or sister. Rose and I couldn't have been happier about our growing family. Joseph Emmett Mackenzie was stillborn at six months. We laid him to rest in the family cemetery, but Rose wasn't the same after that." -Travis's journal

After a short drive that seemed to take forever, Deacon finally pulled into a small gravel parking lot in the middle of nowhere. He jumped out of the truck and slammed his door, coming around the front bumper to open the passenger door and help Amaira down from her seat. She looked at him questioningly, then followed as he turned and headed into a long line of trees without a word. She struggled not to trip over the branches and roots that bordered the steep slope, trying to keep up with him. He moved as if he were a man possessed and the distance between them grew until Deacon had nearly disappeared through a thicket of trees and bushes. Fighting the panic that threatened to choke her at the idea of being abandoned in the woods, Amaira started to run in the direction he'd gone, hoping that he would be in sight again once she breeched the thick copse of trees.

"Easy there," strong hands grabbed her shoulder to stop her before she ran off the edge of a cliff.

"What the Hell, Deacon? First you drag me off into the middle of nowhere, then you leave me behind, and I nearly run right off the face of a cliff! Are you trying to kill me?" Her voice echoed off the rocks as she jabbed at him with a pointed finger, emphasizing every word with a hard poke to his chest. Deacon swore, gently releasing her and shoving his hands in his jean pockets.

"I'm sorry, Amaira. I thought you were right behind me until just a moment ago. I keep forgetting that you're not from around here," he said sincerely, as he looked out over the river below them. "Most folks around here are as familiar with this spot as the back of their hands."

"What are we doing here?" She asked, crossing her arms over her chest.

"This is my favourite place to come when I need to be alone with my thoughts for a bit. It's quiet, and the beauty of the Niagara Escarpment… there's something so peaceful about it. It calms my mind, and everything seems so much clearer when I leave," he explained. "What happened with Layla… that's something that I can't talk about anywhere near my family. I'm sorry you had to witness that at all. No one else knows anything about this."

"So, what's her deal?" Amaira asked. "She doesn't seem like the type of woman to get hung up on a guy."

Deacon snorted with derision.

"I wish that were the case. Everything would be so much simpler if that's all it was," he replied. "I don't even know where to begin."

"How about at the beginning?" She suggested, plopping down on a log as she gazed out over the hills and valleys that stretched out below them. She had to admit, the view from up here was spectacular, and she found herself dreaming of what it would be like in autumn when all the leaves changed colour.

"The beginning…. I guess that would be when my mom and Bruce, the man who raised me, got divorced," he began, taking a seat next to her on the log. "Bruce was a bastard, and I was never happier than the day I found out he wasn't my biological father. He cheated on my mom a lot, called her all kinds of disgusting names, and verbally abused her for years. I hated it. When they got divorced, it surprised everyone that my mom went through with it. In a good way, though. But she spiraled into a depression that scared all of us. I was a kid and didn't quite understand why she was acting so differently. She was withdrawn and sad all the time, didn't eat much either. So, her best friend, Angie, took her on a trip to Mexico. It was a desperate attempt to coax my mom back out her shell, but we were all desperate. That's when she met Alex. You already know the rest, I'm sure. How his ex-girlfriend walked in on them having sex and the whole thing ended up all over the internet? You had to be living under a rock at the time not to know all of that," Deacon rose from his seat and started pacing.

"She was different when she got home. The paparazzi were practically banging down our door, and we even had to move to get away from them, but she was… stronger somehow. I don't really know how to explain it. My mom was back, and she was fighting for herself, for us, again. No one expected Alex to come looking for her. But he did, and he stayed. Anyone who looks at them can tell they love each other. Alex brought my mother back to me, and in the process became this incredible father figure that I looked up too. More so than my real father, because Alex chose to be with us through everything that happened. He fought for us. It's been a source of frustration for many women who've tried to usurp my mom's place in his life and failed. Until Layla that is."

"Are you saying your stepfather cheated on your mother with your ex-girlfriend?" Amaira gasped.

"I'm saying he got her pregnant," Deacon admitted bluntly. "At least… that's what she wants me to think. It would destroy my mom if she ever found out. I can't let that happen, I can't let my sister, or my little brother know any of this… or see her destroyed the way I did. Only it would be so much worse this time."

"I don't understand… why would Alex cheat on your mother?" Amaira frowned. "I've seen how they are together, how much they love each other. That kind of love is what books are written about. It's practically epic."

Deacon grunted, pausing in his pacing to look over at her.

"I don't think he did. I mean… back then I thought he had, and I hated him so much for it. I joined the fucking army to get away from him because I was scared, I would kill him one day. I was in a band when I met Layla, and we were going places. We had gigs all over the country and were in talks with a record label. Layla was gorgeous, and I foolishly believed that it was me she wanted. I made the mistake of bringing her home one weekend and introducing her to my family. A couple months later, she was telling me she was pregnant, and I knew that baby wasn't mine. We'd always used protection, and I had been on the road for weeks. Even if everything failed, the dates didn't match up. I didn't want to be bogged down with a cheating bitch, so I broke it off with her. That's when she told me the baby was Alex's. She told me my mother had invited her for dinner one evening while I was on the road, and that was when Alex seduced her by the pool. My mom was putting my brother and sister to bed. According to Layla, he'd come up behind her and started massaging her shoulders and kissing her neck. She claimed she was completely helpless against his powers of seduction. He fucked her right there beside the pool while his wife and children were in the house. I believed her, but I couldn't allow it to ruin my family. I let her claim her daughter as mine, and for the past ten years, I've been sending her child support, on the condition that she never goes anywhere near my family. Her secret had to stay her secret."

"That's messed up, surely you get that?" Amaira was mind boggled with all the information he'd just shared with her. She didn't believe for a moment that Layla could ever have seduced Alex, but she could believe that the woman had cheated on Deacon and lied through her teeth about it.

"I do now. For years I was blinded by my hurt and anger. I trusted Alex to love my mom, and he'd betrayed that trust. Every time I looked at him, saw his image in magazines, or heard his voice… it re-opened those wounds. I had to leave, so I joined the army and walked away from everything. Then I got injured. I was fleeing from an ambush, when I realized how much of a fool I had been. I let her lies chase me away from my family. My grandfather died while I was in the hospital, but he'd had a stroke a few weeks before and had slipped into a coma. The man who was more of a father to me than anyone else died, and I wasn't here to say goodbye because of her! If she wants to threaten my mother's happiness, she's going to have a hell of a fight on her hands, but I won't let her use me anymore. She's going to have to prove her daughter is Alex's, like my mom did to prove Jack was really mine. DNA is impossible to fake."

Amaira let out a low whistle. She already didn't like the woman, but now, after hearing Deacon's story, she downright hated her.

"What does your girlfriend think about all of this?" Amaira asked.

"What girlfriend?" He asked, puzzled. "I haven't had time for a relationship in years."

"Oh… I'm sorry… that woman coming out of your room the other day… she said… I'm so sorry, it's completely none of my business. Forget I said anything!" She flushed with mortification and wanted to hide under one of the giant boulders littering the cliffside. Deacon laughed.

"I don't really find the humor in this," she muttered.

"The woman coming out of my room, was she tall, blonde and full of attitude?" He asked. When she nodded, he laughed even harder and nearly fell off the log. "She's not my girlfriend. Paris is my nurse. I was sent back here to recuperate after I was injured, but when I heard about my grandfather… as soon as I was out of the Intensive Care Unit, I couldn't stay in that hospital bed any longer, so I signed myself out. My mother insisted on hiring a nurse to check on me from time to time. It was the least I could do to ease her worries."

"You seem quite whole to me. I don't understand why you still need a nurse?" She asked, confusion lacing her voice.

"I must be hiding it better than I thought," Deacon rose to his feet and moved to stand in front of her.

"What are you doing?" She asked, mortified when he started unbuttoning his shirt to reveal washboard abs, that would normally make her drool, covered in gauze and surgical tape. Her mouth formed an "oh," but no sound came out.

Deacon resumed his seat next to her on the log and laced his fingers with hers before bringing them to his lips. She tried to ignore the flames of desire his touch ignited within her from that one simple gesture. She dared not read into it.

"Since you know my relationship status, I think it's only fair that I know yours. Are you seeing anyone?" He asked after a few minutes, changing the subject.

All the air fled from Amaira's lungs as she stared up into his dark blue eyes. She didn't know how long they sat there, staring at each other as she contemplated his words. She wracked her brain for an answer, having suddenly forgotten how to speak.

"I-I'm very single," she shyly admitted. "Much to my mother's annoyance. She's constantly trying to set me up on blind dates, but the only men she knows are ballet dancers, and I've had enough ballet in my life to last a lifetime."

"Do you dance?" He asked, his body inching slightly closer.

"I used too, but I could never be the dancer my mother was. She lived and breathed ballet until she met my father while her ballet company was on tour across the country. She was performing The Nutcracker, and he loved it so much he waited outside the backstage doors to meet her. The tale is more romantic to hear her describe it. Of course, my grandparents were devastated that he chose to marry an American instead of a nice Indian girl, they're very traditional. They refused to attend my parents wedding and barely acknowledge my mother whenever they visit us," Amaira forced herself to stop rambling. Her breath caught in her throat when she noticed Deacon's eyes were locked on her lips.

Without another word, Deacon's mouth came crashing down to hers. The contact sent volts of electricity down her spine, curling her toes inside her boots. As if they had a will of their own, her arms snaked around his shoulders, pulling him closer. Deacon deepened the kiss, their tongues colliding and tangling together as his arms wrapped around her waist and practically pulled her onto his lap. Neither of them heard the crack that should have warned them, seconds before the log collapsed beneath their combined weight, sending them crashing to the ground. Amaira landed on top of Deacon, but she didn't miss the telltale grunts and hissing he released. She scrambled to roll off him, concern outweighing desire as she visually assessed his prone form on the tangle of grass and weeds and pieces of wood.

"Deacon! Are you alright? How's your stomach? Did any stitches break? Deacon?" She asked, forcing away the panic that threatened to choke her as she tried to figure out a way to get help all the way out here, when she didn't have a clue where they were. She dug around in her pocket for her cell phone, relieved to realize that she had enough signal for her GPS to work if she needed it too.

Deacon finally rolled over onto his knees and slowly rose to his feet. He groaned and Amaira rushed to his side, offering what meager support she could to his large frame as he dusted himself off.

"Are you alright?" She asked again.

"Yeah, I think so. Let's head back to the farm. I think I'm going to need some painkillers," he muttered holding his side. Together they managed to pick their way back to his truck. Deacon slammed the gearshift into reverse, backing out of the parking lot and carefully making his way back to the farm.

Chapter 12

"Rose was acting strange for weeks after we lost Joseph. I should have known better than to let her take Sarah grocery shopping with her. I keep asking myself how I could have possibly predicted that Rose would forget her in the hot car. Still, I should have known that something wasn't right. We'd almost lost our only living child because I was willfully blind to Rose's mental deterioration. I missed the Rose I fell in love with. I missed the taste of her lips and the warmth of her embrace." -Travis's journal

His hot breath warmed her skin as his lips and tongue delved into every crevice and tasted every inch of her skin. Amaira writhed beneath him, her hands squeezing and caressing every muscle and plane of his back and ass. And boy did Deacon ever have a great ass! She dimly wondered if she'd be able to bounce a quarter off it. Then he slid between her legs and banished all thought with his tongue. She started trembling, clutching the sheets with her fists, tension coiling low in her abdomen. She couldn't bear it anymore. She was certain he would drive her insane with need, sending her body trembling and shaking harder and harder.

"Amaira," he murmured against her inner thigh, his voice changing as he said her name, becoming higher in pitch. Softer, almost feminine.

"Come on, Amaira. Wake up!"

Amaira bolted upright. She groaned and shut her eyes, collapsing back in bed when she realized she'd been dreaming. She rolled over and buried herself in the comfort of her duvet.

Ignoring Deacon's siblings, however, was nearly impossible to accomplish.

"Why are you waking me up in the middle of the night?" She moaned, pressing her face to her pillow, desperately hoping to fall back asleep.

"It's not the middle of the night, Amaira. It's almost noon!" A creaking of the bedsprings, and a dip in the mattress told her that Deacon's little sister had taken a seat at the corner of her bed.

"Noon? Really?" She opened one eye and peaked over at the old-fashioned alarm clock on her dresser. "Damn, I was having such an incredible dream."

"What was it about?" Tana asked, staring at her innocently.

Amaira blushed, burying her head in the pillow as she mumbled a reply in Hindi.

"What was that? I think the pillow understood you better," Tana teased.

"Oh, leave her alone, Tana! She was clearly dreaming about you-know-who," another voice teased with barely contained laughter.

"You-know-who, eh? Gross," Tana gagged and fell backwards on the bed in a fit of giggles.

Amaira rolled over and threw her pillow at Deacon's sister, mortification warring with amusement. She couldn't decide whether to hide under the blankets or laugh at the girl's antics.

"Come on, Amaira. Please say you'll go camping with us?" Amy begged, adding as an afterthought, "Deacon's coming."

"Yeah, and we need you to distract him, so he doesn't go completely big brother on us tonight," Tana chimed in, batting her eyelashes with mock innocence.

Amaira raised her eyebrow as she took in both girls perched on the foot of her bed. She didn't have sisters, but she did remember what it was like to be a teenage girl with an older brother, and she suspected there was something more going on than a simple family camping trip.

"Well… I don't need a distraction but Amy…" Tana descended into a riot of giggles again as Amy smacked her with a pillow and shoved her off the bed. She shouted breathlessly from the floor, "Amy has a boyfriend who's going to be there."

"Montana shut up! He's not my boyfriend," Amy squeaked, using her sister's full name, her face and neck turning a bright red. Amaira laughed.

"I see. You need me to go camping with you so I can distract Deacon while you sneak off into the bushes with your 'not boyfriend.'" Amaira surmised, sitting up in bed and stretching. "I'm not really sure I'm the right person for that. I'm far too responsible to go camping with a bunch of teenagers and loose track of them. Haven't you ever seen a horror movie? It's always the horny teenagers that get killed first."

"Last time I checked, there weren't any Freddy Kreuger's hanging around these parts. Amy argued, smiling.

"Touché," Amaira murmured. "I still don't feel comfortable with it."

"We're not going to do anything. Our entire family will be there, it would be suicide. It's just that… we're both going off to college soon and I wanted a chance to talk to him before senior year started, that's all. It's not at all like Tana insinuated. I'm not my mom," Amy assured her.

"Hey! That's my dad you're talking about," Tana mimed vomiting as she climbed back onto the bed.

"I am so confused right now," Amaira's attention darted back and forth between the girls.

"My mom," Amy began.

"And my dad," Tana continued.

"Were best friends since birth, and when they were our age," Amy said.

76

"They thought they were in love," Tana replied.

"They had unprotected sex," Amy explained.

"And that resulted in Deacon," Tana finished, sparking a memory of Jack relaying that exact tale a few days earlier over a cup of coffee.

"But I'm not like that," Amy said. "Nathan and I hated each other for years and our mom's have been best friends since high school. Aunt Angie was even the driving force behind mom going to Mexico and meeting my dad. She won the tickets for the trip on some radio contest and dragged my mom along with her. Anyways, last year Nathan and I started dating. My parents know, but Deacon doesn't yet, and I wanted to talk to Nathan first before he found out. I don't know how Deacon's going to react. All our families will be there though. Come on, I swear it'll be more fun than it sounds. Please?"

"Plus, you'll get some first-hand experience with our parents for your script," Tana cajoled.

"And you'll finally be able to meet my little brother, Riley. He returned from his visit with my grandmother. We picked him up at the airport yesterday and the first thing he wanted to do, after meeting you, was go on a camping trip," Amy mentioned.

Amaira groaned and fell back on her pillow. She didn't know the first thing about camping. What was she going to tell her boss when he inevitably asked her how the script was coming along? She was probably going to be fired from her dream job, since all she has so far are notes that she'd quickly jotted down in her notebook. This was going to be one hell of an experience for her.

～～

"When you said we were going camping, I pictured at least leaving the farm," Amaira commented as they trekked towards the woods and shoreline bordering it.

77

"We normally do, but with Deacon still recovering from his injuries, mom decided we needed to stay close to home. You know, in case something happens, or it ends up being too much for him." Amy replied with a shrug.

Amaira nodded in understanding, and quietly took in their surroundings. The sky was blue, the trees were a mix of blooming and budding, and the ground was no longer muddy from melting snow. She breathed a sigh of relief that her shoes weren't going to be sucked into another muddy abyss, the latest victim of nature versus fashion. They reached their destination and Deacon set down his rucksack in a large clearing near the edge of the lake and surrounded by a thick ring of trees that bordered a heavily wooded area. The large group followed his lead and set down their belongings in a pile near the centre of the clearing.

"Hey Jack, let's start setting up the tents. I'm thinking over here looks like a nice dry spot," Xander practically shouted at the larger man as he indicated the area behind him. Jack grunted, kissed his wife, and ambled over to him. Amaira watched in fascination as they started pulling out poles and canvas and started constructing a rather large, blue tent. She pulled out her notebook and a pen and jotted down a few quick observations as she watched, plopping down on a boulder as she got lost in her work.

"Amaira, come help us find some wood for the fire," Deacon's brother, Riley, slung his arm around her shoulder and steered her towards the woods. He was tall like his older brother, but leaner, with dark hair that curled over the tops of his ears. "It will be great to get to know you better. I've heard so much about you."

"Riley, I could use your help preparing the area for our bonfire," Deacon called out before they could get too far. The lanky teen smirked at her and winked, reminding her of a much younger version of his famous father. She had little doubt that he was going to be as much of a heartbreaker as his father had been before he'd married Sarah.

"We were just about to do that big brother," Riley grinned cockily and kept walking.

"Get your ass over here, Squirt," Deacon commanded. "Let the girls collect sticks and help me build a firepit."

"But who will protect them if they run into a bear?" Riley protested.

"Bears?" Amaira choked, warily eyeing the forest, and wishing she was back in the safety of the farmhouse.

"Oh puh-leeze, like you wouldn't run away screaming like a little baby if you came face to face with a real bear," Amy teased, grabbing Amaira's hand and leading her away. "Come on, Amaira. Don't let this dolt scare you. I've never seen any bears around here."

Amaira swallowed the lump in her throat and forced herself to put one foot in front of the other as she followed Amy and Tana into the woods. She could hear Deacon and Riley as they continued to argue with each other, but the farther they went into the woods, the quieter the voices became.

"I'm sorry about Riley," Amy murmured as she bent to pick up some sticks. "I should have warned you."

"He's always looking for a way to get under Deacon's skin," Tana quipped from a few feet away.

Amaira simply nodded, not sure what to say, and went to work gathering sticks and bits of wood for the campfire. When their arms were full, the trio headed back to the campsite. Tents of various sizes were set up in a semi-circle facing the lake. The view was simply breathtaking, and she stood there taking it all in. She couldn't help but look forward to the sunset, wondering if it would be as spectacular as the view she was currently enjoying. Deacon took the armful of sticks from her and began building a pyramid in the center of a large shallow hole, surrounded by a thick ring of stones.

"What are you doing?" She couldn't help but ask.

"I'm getting the fire ready," he replied.

"Don't worry," Riley piped up, once again slinging an arm around her shoulders. He winked conspiratorially at her. "If Deeks can't get the fire going, I'll keep you warm."

Before anyone had a chance to respond, Xander dumped a large bottle of water on his son's head. Amaira laughed, even as some of the cold water splashed her. She still couldn't get used to thinking of him as Alex.

"What was that for?" Riley sputtered indignantly, letting her go so he could face his father.

"You looked like you could use a cold shower," Xander replied.

She couldn't help it. She tried so hard not to laugh, but the sound simply bubbled out of her until she was practically in tears. Riley yanked his shirt off and tossed it at her, leaving a giant wet print in the middle of her chest and surprising her. He chuckled and darted into one of the tents before Deacon could take two steps towards them. Deacon glanced at the tent with amusement before making his way over to her.

"Are you alright? Sorry about my lame ass brother. Kid might have his dad's looks, but he's got no game," Deacon joked softly.

"I'm fine," she answered honestly. "I think he was trying to get a rise out of you more than anything else."

"You're probably right," he replied with a grin. "Come on, I'll get the fire going so you can dry off."

"It's alright, Deeks. We've got this," Amy and Tana slipped an arm around each of Amaira's and led her away to the stony shore before anyone could protest. Enveloped in the welcoming warmth of the sun, Amaira sighed and yanked her sweater off. She spread it on the rocks to dry and followed the girls down to the water's edge. Across the lake, she could make out what looked to be an old stone fortress. Curious, she asked about it.

"That's Fort Niagara in New York," Tana answered. "You can't see it well from here, but over there is Fort George, which was built and controlled by the British before Canada was a country of its own. During the war of 1812, the two Fortresses were constantly firing canons at each other, since they were so close together, until the Americans decided to try and invade."

Amaira stared at Tana, stunned by the amount of information she'd shared.

"What?" Tana asked, shrugging. "I like history."

"Tana's planning on majoring in it when she goes to University in a few years," Amy explained.

"Wow, I'm impressed," Amaira exclaimed. "Are you planning to be a history teacher someday?"

"I haven't decided yet. I might go into museum studies and be a curator somewhere." Tana picked up a stone and tossed it into the lake, skipping it across the water before it finally sank.

"That's great," Amaira smiled at her.

Tana shrugged, picking up another stone and tossing it. Amy sat on the shore, stretching her legs, and letting the waves lap at her toes. She turned her face towards the sun, blissfully shutting her eyes as she soaked up the sunlight. Amaira sat next to her, ignoring the rocks poking into her legs.

"Mom and Nathan's family should be arriving soon with the food. They're driving down to the edge of the woods and carrying the coolers from there. Then we'll probably start roasting marshmallows and all that fun stuff. Have you figured out how to distract Deacon yet?" Amy asked.

"I'm still not entirely convinced I should," Amaira replied. "How long do I need to distract him for, and how far away are the two of you going to be?"

"We'll probably come down here and take a short, romantic stroll along the water," Amy sighed.

"At sunset," Tana supplied. "It's always the most romantic time in the movies."

Amaira chuckled at the exaggerated expression on Tana's face as she batted her eyelashes and sighed. Amy shot her a disgruntled look. Amaira swore she heard a muttered "so immature," and shared a conspiratorial grin with Tana.

"I have a better idea," Amaira offered. "Why don't we go as a group. Tana and I can walk a small distance apart from the two of you so you can have your privacy, and Deacon wouldn't suspect a thing."

"That wont work. He'd probably try to join us. Haven't you noticed how he watches you sometimes? There's so much heat in his gaze I'm surprised you haven't spontaneously combusted," Amy teased.

The sound of a car horn nearby stopped Amaira from speaking what was on the tip of her tongue. Amy clapped her hands and took off without another word, leaving her and Tana to stare at her receding form. Sighing, they shared sympathetic eye rolls and headed after her.

Chapter 13

*"It was love at first sight... I just didn't know it yet. I was a
fool back then, but smart enough to know that Rose was a woman
I couldn't live without. It took losing her to realize how much I
loved her. I'd give anything to have her back. I can only hope our
daughter and maybe someday grandchildren, aren't so blind to
it." – Travis's Journal*

The woods were bathed in the orange and gold glow of the
campfire. Flickering flames caused the shadows to move and
dance as if they were alive. For the first time in weeks, Deacon
was completely at peace. Watching Amaira as she talked openly
with his mother and sisters and laughing at Riley's antics to
garner her attention, he was struck with a suddenly overwhelming
sense of... something. Deacon shook his head to clear it of his
wayward thoughts. It couldn't be love. Right? He didn't believe it
existed for him. This sensation filling his chest, however,
whenever she smiled was completely foreign to him. What else
could it be? He didn't subscribe to his mother's belief in love at
first sight. Yet, since the moment she arrived, Amaira had
claimed a piece of him. He couldn't decide on the actual moment
when it had happened, but now that he acknowledged it, Deacon
realized she had been in his heart from their very first meeting. It
was about time he did something about it, he decided and slowly
rose from his chair. He caught her eye as he approached, and with
a grin, he held his hand out in invitation. She slipped her small
hand in his and rose to her feet, standing mere inches away from
him. Turning, Deacon led her away from the campfire and the
zillion eyes watching their every move.

"See Riley, that's what real game looks like," Tana teased as they reached the edge of the woods. Deacon chuckled and looked behind them to see his little brother gaping at them like a fish out of water.

"B-b-but he didn't even say a word. How did he do that?" Riley sputtered. His dad simply clapped him on the shoulder in a sympathetic gesture that had the rest of the group howling with laughter like a pack of wild animals.

"Come on," Deacon gently tugged on Amaira's hand. She smiled shyly back at him and followed his lead, picking their way through twigs and over fallen branches in the growing darkness so far from the glow of the fire. The silence between them was almost as thick as the wooded night. Deacon trusted his memory of the land and his heightened senses to guide them through it until their feet landed on the rocky shore. Moonlight glistened off the rippling water, as they kicked off their shoes and strolled along the lake, letting the waves lap at their toes.

"I'm sorry if I embarrassed you back there. My family can be a little bit...." Deacon struggled to find the right words, but the harder he tried the more elusive they became.

"It's fine. My family can be a little difficult sometimes too," Amaira waved off his apology. Silence descended around them once more as they enjoyed the breeze and the sound of an owl hooting from a nearby tree combining with the sounds of the lake lapping at the shore.

"The stars are so beautiful here. I've never seen so many in once place before," Amaira gushed, her head tilted back to admire the night sky.

"Yeah, they're beautiful alright. But they don't hold a candle to the view I'm looking at," Deacon quietly murmured.

Surprised, Amaira faced him, a slow smile spread across her face. He couldn't resist reaching out to smooth the silken strands of her hair back, tucking them behind her ear. His hand travelled over her shoulder to the base of her neck as he lowered his head to hers.

The contact of her lips sent sparks of electricity through his body, and he hungrily deepened the kiss. Amaira let out a little sigh as he parted her lips, his tongue invading her mouth in exploration. She pressed her body against his, pulling him down to his knees and ignoring the rocks that bit into their flesh as they consumed one another. Deacon's hands slid down her back, searching for the hem of her shirt, and slipped beneath it. Before he could enjoy the feel of her warm skin beneath his calloused hands, Amaira was eagerly yanking at his shirt, pulling it up and over his head to toss it in a heap by their feet. He sucked in a breath at the sensation of her warm palms on his abdomen, relishing in the contact as it burned into his flesh.

"Where are your bandages?" Amaira broke their kiss, staring at the angry looking red scar beneath her fingers.

"They were removed this morning. I don't need them anymore," Deacon replied, lacing his fingers through hers.

"Amazing," Amaira murmured, and he was instantly distracted by the heat of her palm on his abdomen. He kissed her again, pulling her closer. Before he realized what was happening, she sank to her knees in front of him, kissing the line down his chest and stomach muscles.

"Absolutely incredible, Deacon," she murmured as she pressed a gentle kiss to his scar, her hands sliding down to the waistband of his jeans and slipping the button open. His body warmed with desire as she unzipped his pants and slowly eased them down to his knees, his erection springing free from its confinement and standing proud in the light of the moon.

"Amaira," he whispered softly, his hands burying into her hair as her tongue skimmed along the length of his arousal. He watched as she slipped her free hand down along her belly and beneath the band of her pants. Her tongue twirled around the silken tip of his penis teasingly, as her fingers teased her core. A soft moan escaped her lips as they parted to his gentle invasion.

All thought vanished as she worked her oral magic on him. His hips thrust with her rhythm; his groans filling the air around them. Deacon thrust deeper into her mouth, touching the back of her throat as she massaged his balls with her free hand. She swallowed, her throat contracting around him. He tried to go slow and be gentle with her. To take his time. But she was greedy and demanding, picking up her pace as she continued to pleasure herself as well. He could feel the moment she came, her mouth releasing him with a pop. He watched as she greedily fingered herself, taking his cock into his fist and pumping. She grabbed her breast, as she convulsed, and he came all over the beach.

Deacon ran a hand through his golden hair, then reached down to help her to her feet, but instead Amaira took his hand and pulled him down next to her. He grunted as his knee connected with the hard ground. Amaira pulled him closer, and smoothed back his hair, allowing him to gently ease her onto her back. Deacon trailed kisses down her throat, the brush of his lips against the sensitive flesh reigniting the flame that burned low in her belly. Her breasts tingled with anticipation, her nipples turning to hard pebbles beneath hands that lightly brushed against them. Amaira barely noticed the rocks under her back, she didn't care that anyone could happen upon them. All she wanted was this moment with him to last forever, his hands on her body, his mouth wreaking havoc on her senses until she could no longer tell where he ended, and she began. When he pulled her nipple into his mouth and rolled it between his teeth, she gasped with pleasure, arching into him, searching for more. Deacon, sensing her restlessness, unclasped her bra and freed her from its confinements, tossing it aside as his mouth continued its delightful torture. Skimming his hands down her sides, he slowly restoked the fire inside her, sending her spiraling into an abyss.

"Deacon!" She called out breathlessly. "I need you. Please. I want you inside me."

Deacon paused his ministrations, his gaze resting on her belly button. The heat of his breath on her skin made her shiver with excitement. Panting, she gazed up at the night sky as it sparkled with a million diamonds, when she realized his pause was a little too long.

"Deacon?" She asked, struggling to sit up as he pulled away from her. Amaira covered herself, shyness creeping over her with the growing distance between them.

"Deacon? What's wrong?" Amaira watched as he rose to his feet, jerkily yanking his boxers and jeans back up over his hips. Wordlessly, he took a couple steps and retrieved their discarded clothing. Handing her shirt and bra over, Amaira pulled her top over her head, and shoved her bra in her pocket. Confusion, and hurt warred inside her heart. Did she do or say something wrong? Tears pooled in the corners of her eyes.

"Amaira," he softly whispered her name, and it was then that she realized he was standing in front of her, fully clothed and watching her with a nameless expression on his face.

"I just... I don't understand what's happening right now," she turned and stormed off in the direction they had come, hoping the sting of his rejection would fade before she reached camp and had a million eyes on her again.

"Amaira! Wait!" Deacon shouted, racing to catch up with her. "Would you stop for a minute and listen?"

Furious, Amaira whipped around and faced him, ready to give him a piece of her mind, but he cut her off before she had the chance.

"Do you really want our first time together to be some hurried fuck a few steps away from my entire family? I don't. I plan to take my time with you," he stepped closer until he was barely an inch away from her, forcing Amaira to look up at him and making her heart race. "You deserve better, and I plan on making it worth the wait. Amaira, you're incredible. What you did was… mind-blowing. I had no idea that was going to happen when I brought you out here for a romantic stroll. But I want more than some meaningless quickie. When I make you scream, and I promise, you will scream, I don't want you holding back because someone might hear us. When you weep, it'll be with pleasure. When I finally fuck you, Amaira, I want your every orgasm to scramble your brains until you forget your own name."

Deacon's fingers tucked a loose strand of hair behind her ear as he lowered his head to hers. Pausing before their lips touched, he whispered her name before taking her mouth and using his tongue to show her exactly what he intended to do to her.

Chapter 14

"I pray my daughter never suffers the way I have. Loosing someone you love isn't easy but opening yourself to love after loss is a difficult thing to do. It's damn near impossible to do with a farm to run and a daughter to raise. Not everyone's lucky enough to get a second chance, so I'll teach her to hold onto it for dear life if it ever comes her way. I owe her that much. I only wish Rose had held onto me like that." -Travis's journal.

"So, how's the script coming along?" Sarah asked, taking a seat next to Amaira around the smoldering campfire the next morning.

"I hope my son hasn't been distracting you from your work," she murmured, blushing as she turned her gaze towards the hot embers as Piper tried to breathe life back into the flames with tinder and newspaper.

"N-no, he's been trying to help me, but it's kind of hard since he doesn't know the entire story behind your romance with Xander," Amaira stammered awkwardly.

"I see," Sarah nodded, as if affirming something to herself before continuing. "I'm sorry about that. It can't be easy trying to write a story about someone who's been completely absent from the narrative. Between Deacon's injuries and my father's passing... I'm sorry. I haven't been myself lately. I know Jack's told you part of the story, and I'm sure Deacon has as well. I'll do my best to fill in the holes."

"Thank you," Amaira grabbed her notebook and pen from her bag next to her chair, ready to start jotting notes as Sarah told her the story of how she and Xander met and fell-in-love. It wasn't in Mexico where they first met, or even when she discovered she was pregnant with Amy weeks later, that she realized she'd fallen in love with him. It was the night he appeared at her best-friend's wedding, his heart on his sleeve in front of her friend's and family, that she knew but was too scared at the time to fully admit it to herself. So much was changing in her life, and she was terrified of the biggest change of all. Loving a charming, wonderful man who held the power to hurt her more than Jack or her ex-husband ever could. Sarah explained how Xander stood by her side, patiently supporting her, and immediately accepting of the fact that she was pregnant with his child. He never once doubted her claims, as some in his position would have. Especially after finding out that that's exactly what had happened with Deacon, albeit unintentionally. His strength and support gave her the courage to go after what she wanted, to fight for herself for the first time in her life. Amaira sniffed, imagining the beauty and tragedy of their romance as Sarah spoke. She understood now why Xander had been so hesitant about her writing this story. Nothing she wrote could ever do this love justice, especially on screen.

Sarah paused, frowning as her attention flickered between the fire and Amaira as if debating something with herself. Amaira watched, fascinated at the myriad of expressions crossing the other woman's face, curious what she might have to say.

"My son... I hope you aren't using him to get closer to my family, or to my husband. I know it's happened in the past, and he's been hurt a lot," Sarah sucked in a deep breath to steady herself, but Amaira cut her off before she could finish.

"You're son's a grown man. I think he can handle having a relationship without his mother interfering. No offense, I'm sure you mean well, but my interest in your son has nothing to do with you or your husband," Amaira's cheeks burned. She bent and

90

shoved her notes in the backpack Tana had loaned her, her movements jerky as she struggled not to say anything else and stood. Sarah stopped her with a gesture, and Amaira plopped back down in her folding chair, crossing her arms defensively over her chest. It hurt like hell that Deacon's mother would plop her in the same category as that bitch Layla. But she reluctantly understood Sarah's guarded questions about her intentions.

"Amaira, you have no idea how much I needed to hear you say those words," Sarah murmured softly, a single tear escaping from the corner of her eye. "He might not admit it, but my son has been hurt so many times by women with ulterior motives. The last one... well... let's not get started on Layla. She was the straw that broke the camel's back so to speak. Anyways, what I was trying to say is that my son might seem all hard and tough on the outside, but he's soft and loveable on the inside. Takes after my father that way. He's a different man now than when he left, but there's still a bit of softness left in him. I can see it in the way he looks at you. You, Amaira, have the power to hurt him more than any other woman ever could. Just like Alex has that power over me. Please, be careful with him."

"The last thing I would ever wish to do, Mrs. Hawkins, is hurt your son," Amaira reluctantly tried to reassure her.

"Thank you," Sarah replied.

"Are we all done with the protective mama bear show now?" Piper piped in, plopping down on the ground between them as if she were younger than her nearly 50 years. Sarah nodded and Piper grinned back at them both. "Good. Now, while the kiddos are all off fishing with the He-Men lets finalize some of these details for the party next week."

"Party?" Amaira asked, her brow furrowing in confusion.

"Mm-hmm. Didn't the girls tell you? That's why we needed you to distract Deacon for a bit last night. Since he hasn't been home for his birthday in ten years, and it's his dirty thirty, we've been busy planning a super secret surprise birthday bash for him. Why do you look so surprised? Montana and Amy didn't say anything did they?" Piper asked, rolling her eyes to the clouds, and muttering about saving her from her mischievous teenage daughter.

"If I recall, Montana's not half as bad as you were at that age," Sarah laughed. "Not sharing our secrets with a guest… that's actually pretty tame considering what you were getting up too."

Piper groaned, prostrating herself on the ground and covering her eyes with her hands. It took Amaira a moment to realize that Piper's groans had turned into a fit of giggles, and she laughed at the sight of Deacon's stepmother rolling around in the dirt bemoaning the trouble with teenage girls.

"Ignore the drama queen down there. If the girls didn't tell you about the party. What did they tell you?" Sarah asked, watching her curiously.

"Well… ummm… I believe there was a story involving Nathan and Amy dating," Amaira began guiltily sharing what she hoped wasn't an actual secret now that she knew the truth about the girls need for a distraction last night.

"Did I hear you say that Nathan and Amy are dating?" Sarah's friend Angie was beautifully timeless with her raven black hair and not a single wrinkle that Amaira could spot. Having seen her and Sarah together around the campfire, it wasn't difficult for Amaira to picture them causing trouble together in a foreign country and capturing the attention of a Hollywood Hunk.

"That's what the girls told me anyway," Amaira admitted.

"He hasn't said anything to us yet, but I'm pretty sure my son's gay," Angie casually confessed. "I accidentally opened up one of his super secret computer files, which I am never doing again by the way! I learned far more than I ever wanted too about male anatomy in that one short video. I hate all this tiptoeing around in our house though, I wish he'd just come out of that

92

damn closet already and stop sneaking around like a horny cat or something. I mean, what's he afraid of exactly?"

"You win," Piper pitched in, having reclaimed her seat between Amaira and Sarah, a twig tangled in her blond hair. "I thought teenage girls were bad, but that… that sucks. Nothing worse than when your kid keeps some giant secret life like that from you."

"Really? You just had to dig that hole a little deeper didn't you Piper?" Sarah teased, opening her mouth to say more, just as the men returned from the lake with their fishing poles.

"Dig what hole deeper?" Deacon asked, his eyes darting between his mother and stepmother before coming to rest on Amaira.

"From what I understand, the ladies are trading barbs on who was the worst teenager. Piper for being so mischievous, or Sarah for keeping secrets. Did I get that right?" Amaira asked, glancing at Sarah for confirmation.

"Really? And have you come to a decision?" Angie's husband Greg asked curiously as he leaned his fishing pole against a tree.

"Not really. I don't think I have enough information, but perhaps you guys would like to weigh in?" Amaira ignored the flutters in her abdomen as Deacon's laughing gaze landed on her and warmed.

"Well, if you ask me," he began.

"It was definitely," Jack piped in at the same time.

"Sarah," all four men answered in unison.

Sarah gaped at them, as Piper cackled gloatingly.

"How… how can you all say I was worse? Alex, you didn't even know me back then! And Deacon, you traitor, I'm your mother!" Sarah sputtered with mock indignation, barely able to contain the grin that Amaira could see forming on her lips. Amaira grinned quickly jotting down notes in her book as the guys settled around the campfire with them. Xander… no, Alex, she reminded herself for the thousandth time… sat next to his wife, rubbing her back in consolation, and whispering something in her ear that made Sarah blush profusely. Yep, those two were still madly in love with each other Amaira decided. Her gaze drifted over to Deacon, watching him as he stoked the fire and added another log, and wondered if she might find that same kind of love some day. The kind of love that writers wrote about, and dreamers could only dream of.

She understood her parents a lot more now, she realized, and how they were able to keep their marriage strong in the face of so many obstacles. It couldn't have been easy for them after her grandparents condemned the match and refused to have anything to do with them until Amaira and her brother had been much older. Only then, it was because they wanted to know their grandchildren. They still never fully embraced her parents love match, or the fact that her mother wasn't Indian. Her grandmother especially was far too traditional and had always believed her son would settle into a nicely arranged marriage with the daughter of a friend of hers from India, despite having immigrated to California before he was even born. A marriage much like their own. Her grandparents adored one another, and Amaira had always longed for that kind of attachment. She was also starting to understand her parents' defiance of tradition and their insistence that they fell in love at first sight. Glancing over at Deacon, her heart warmed and beat faster when his gaze locked on hers. She was beginning to believe in it too.

Chapter 15

"There are so many things I miss about Rose. Her heart, her soul, her laughter… but most of all I miss her passion. Rose was passionate about so many things: nature; children; her favourite books. I hold the memories close to my heart. No one else could ever taste her passion the way I had or miss the warmth of her body flush from making love. She was my passion, my heart." - Travis's journal

Amaira dumped her stuff in her room and snatched a towel from the closet. She bumped into Deacon on the way to the shower and tried to ignore the flush of her cheeks as she passed him. His hand on her arm, froze her on the spot but she refused to turn around and face him, afraid he would recognize her heart in her eyes and run away.

Amaira shook his hand off and excused herself as she stepped into the bathroom. Deacon stopped her from shutting the door behind her with a foot in the jamb, holding it open.

"What are you doing?" She asked breathlessly.

Deacon moved so quickly she didn't have a chance to get away. In a blur of movement, she found herself pinned to the wall by his body, his hot breath warming her ear.

"What are you doing?" She whispered, surprised by the low timber of it.

"I was planning to do something romantic for our first time together, but apparently I'm not that patient," he replied with a huskiness in his voice that had her heart racing. She was speechless as his mouth descended on hers, possessing her. His tongue traced her lips before invading her mouth and silencing any protest she might have made if his touch didn't completely liquify her brain. Not that she would have.

He released her hands, skimming his own down her body and igniting every nerve in their path. Amaira gasped, reaching for the hem of his shirt. Deacon stopped her hands, holding them both above her head with one of his large ones. His other hand kneaded her ass, molding it with his strong grip. Groaning, he dropped her hands as he urged first one leg, then the next around his waist, holding her up as he grinded against her.

"Deacon," she gasped, arching into him, searching for more contact, and cursing the barrier of their clothes.

His lips claimed hers, as he swirled his hips against her core, swallowing the sounds she made. He lifted her away from the wall, her legs locked around his body, and carried her into another room. She dimly heard water running and tore her attention away long enough to see they were in the bathroom, and he'd started the shower. Deacon continued trailing his lips down her throat and along the collar of her shirt. Setting her down, he reached for the hem of her t-shirt and pulled it up over her head.

"I want you," his voice was husky with desire. "In case I wasn't clear enough, I'm going to show you how much I want you, again and again until it's seared in your brain and on your body."

Quickly stripping each other, Deacon lifted her into the tub and followed her, pressing his hard body against hers and igniting every blood cell in her veins. Amaira reached down to circle his large cock with her fingers, but he pinned her against the wall instead, steam rising around them as hot water pelted their bodies. Grabbing the soap bottle, he squirted the liquid across her breasts, grinding his hips against her.

"You have no idea how much I enjoyed watching you pleasure yourself last night," he groaned against her ear. "It's been playing in my head on repeat all day."

Deacon squeezed her breasts, his hands kneaded the soap into bubbles, gliding all over her body before turning her and pressing her against the cold, tiled wall. Amaira let out a little mew of protest before she pressed her bottom into him moaning with pleasure from the slickness of their bodies moving together. Deacon lifted her leg, setting her foot on the edge of the tub. His hands slid down the front of her body and around to her ass, spreading her cheeks to give him access to her. The tip of his erection slid against her, and the sensation filled her vision with stars. He nipped her shoulders as he moved his hips in a circular motion, making her gasp as he teased her. She arched into him, searching for more as her breasts pressed into the hard tile, but he held her still with one large, calloused hand on her hip. His other hand slipped between her and the wall, opening her and sliding his fingers around her clit, making her beg for more as her body clenched around him, his mouth devouring the nape of her neck and shoulder. It was too much. She couldn't possibly handle any more of this tension coiling through her body. When his other hand released her hip and skimmed up her body, he took her breast in his grip and molded it, squeezed it, and pinched the nipple. The tightness in her lower abdomen released and she came on him, the world shattering around her.

Dimly, she became aware of the heat pelting her body, the shower washing away the last remnants of the soap Deacon had used. His movements had slowed, soothing her at the same time as they began to restoke the fire inside her. She tried to turn towards him, but he kept her pinned against the wall with his body.

"Deacon," she called out shakily. "I want... I want...."

"I know exactly what you want," he growled in her ear, making her pulse skip a beat. He turned her around, pressing her back into the wall as he lowered his mouth to her breast. He sucked a nipple into his mouth, rolling it between his teeth as he nipped and sucked, his hand mimicking his mouth with her other breast. Amaira was helpless with the blinding need that coursed through her body. She couldn't help but whimper when he released her breasts to nip and lick his way down her body. She laced her fingers through his hair as his mouth latched onto her core, his lips mimicking what they'd done to her breast. Her body shook, and her legs threatened to give way beneath her, until Deacon was the only thing holding her up. He growled possessively against her already sensitive flesh, the vibration sending her over the edge.

"Yes," she cried with her second release. "Yes. Yes!"

Deacon moved up the length of her body when she stopped trembling, pressing his flesh against her as he wrapped her legs around his body. He turned off the water and carried her limp body out into the hallway. Amaira buried her face in his shoulder, inhaling the scent of his skin as he moved and shivered with the cold air that stung her heated flesh.

"Where are you taking me?" she quietly asked.

"To find the nearest condom before I lose myself in you," he responded, carrying her into his bedroom.

Depositing her on his bed, still soaking wet, Amaira wiggled into the middle of it while he opened a drawer and pulled out a silver package. Tearing it open with his teeth, he fisted his erection, pumping himself as he rolled the condom down it's length. It was the hottest thing Amaira could remember ever seeing, and she skimmed her hands over her breasts and down her body as she watched. Deacon growled, climbing over her, but he didn't stop her movements, instead watching her as he continued pumping himself. She writhed beneath him, watching their movements as they pleasured themselves. She couldn't believe how bold she was acting, but she was helpless to stop herself. Something about him brought out the boldness and passion inside her. Her back arching off the bed, Deacon dropped down to kiss her, plunging into her body at the same time. Her body clenched around his cock as he moved deeper inside her body, stretching her with his length as he slowly moved, his rhythm and pace increasing deliciously when she cried for more. Harder and faster when she begged for it. With every thrust he brought her closer and closer to the edge until she spiraled over it again, this time dragging him along with her.

Eventually, Amaira slowly came back to her senses, languishing with the pleasure of Deacon's large body still pressing hers into the mattress. She couldn't remember sex ever being so intense before and wondered if it was different this time because the man above her owned her heart in a way no one else ever had. Freezing at the thought, Amaira pondered it for a moment and smiled. He might not know it yet, and she was in no rush to share it with him, but there could never be anyone else for her. She loved Deacon, and everything about him.

Chapter 16

"I took Sarah down to the willow tree. We had a picnic together as we enjoyed the sunshine and the lake. Rose had loved this place so much, I spread her ashes there. Sarah doesn't know it, but her mother was with us that day. I could feel her around us with every kiss of the gentle breeze. For the first time since she passed, I finally felt at peace. I hope this place might also help Sarah find peace someday." -Travis's journal

"I have a whole list of things I need to do today. Any chance you can give me a ride into town? That is, if the farm can do without you for a few hours?" Amaira asked hopefully, as she bounded into the kitchen. She grabbed an apple out of the fruit bowl on the scarred kitchen table and took a giant, juicy bite, savouring the tartness on her tongue.

"Since spring is over, and it isn't quite time to harvest anything yet, I think I can spare a few hours," Deacon replied as he moved around the counter that separated them and wrapped an arm around her waist.

He pulled her backwards against his hard body and brushed his lips along the nape of her neck. Amaira shivered with delight and tried to twist around in his arms as he held her firmly against him. His scent assailed her as his lips wreaked havoc on her body. She let out a little moan, grinding her backside against him. It had been a week since they'd started sharing a bed, and she still couldn't get enough of him. She'd resorted to writing and jotting down notes when he was out in the orchard. Deacon was far too distracting for her to attempt to write when he was around.

"Although... it is my birthday today. I've got something better than running errands in mind for the next few hours," the low,

100

sensuous tones of his voice washed over her. Amaira's knees were weak as she struggled to remember the plan today to keep him busy and far away from the farm while his family set up for the party tonight.

"Come on Deacon. Stop playing games with me. It's not fair and I have stuff to do," Amaira bit her lip. "Do I need to google the area and drive myself around to get it done?"

Deacon groaned, reluctantly releasing her from his grasp. Amaira stepped away, reluctantly putting a little distance between them and took a moment to regain control of her wantonness.

"Alright, what is it that you need to do?" He asked gruffly, raking a hand through his hair. Amaira grinned, grabbing her purse and taking his hand to tug him along with her.

"First, I need to find you a birthday gift," she winked at him and grinned when he groaned and followed her out the door.

Examining the area, Amaira took a deep, calming breath, relief filling her at the lack of evidence of a party or people as they returned to the farm. Gravel crunched under the tires of Deacon's truck as he pulled to a stop in front of the house.

"I'm going to go slip into something a little more comfortable," she wiggled her eyebrows comically, which made him chuckle. "Then I thought we could take a stroll through the orchard while the sun sets? I'd love to hear you sing under the stars again."

"That's really what you want to do, after making me watch you try on sexy lingerie all morning?" He blew out a breath of frustration, clearly struggling to maintain his control.

Amaira was rather impressed with the control he's had over himself all day. She'd pulled every trick she could think of to try and break it. She'd come close to breaking several times, tempted to drag him into a change room or dark alley as they'd explored downtown. Before she could lose control of herself again, Amaira jumped out of the truck with her bags and jogged up the steps to the house. She would have to wait until tonight, and she prayed she'd be able to control herself until then. The man would have to be made of steel to resist her teasing the entire day. An hour later, she was dressed in a slinky summer dress, her hair styled in a mass of curls down her back. Deacon turned, his gaze burning a whole through her as he slowly perused her body, stopping at her feet.

"Are you sure you want to go for a stroll through the orchard in those?" He asked incredulously as he took in her sexiest pair of black stilettos. "I could always sing for you here. Maybe with those sexy legs wrapped around my waist all night."

"Easy tiger," she let out a low, husky laugh. "Maybe you could show me around the barn first. I still haven't seen it."

"The barn huh?" He smirked. "I should have known that's where it would be. Lead the way, Sugar."

"Where what would be?" Amaira asked, the blood draining from her face as butterflies swarmed her stomach.

"The surprise party," Deacon replied, practically strutting to the door with an arrogance that surprised her.

"Surprise party?" She froze in shock. How had he figured it out? She was positive she hadn't let anything slip.

"My family were a little too obviously absent today," he answered from the doorway. Amaira started, she hadn't realized she had spoken out loud. With his reply, she let out the breath she was holding. "Don't worry. I'll be sure to act surprised, but you and me? We aren't finished tonight. As soon as this party's over, you're all mine Amaira. You're all I want for my birthday, and I plan on unwrapping you as slowly as possible. Consider it your penance for keeping secrets from me."

Deacon winked and dashed out the door before she had a chance to reply. Once Amaira recovered her wits, she dashed after him, desperate to catch up to him without twisting an ankle in her strappy black stilettos. But he was nowhere in sight. She searched everywhere as she headed towards the barn, and nearly screamed when a hand reached out from inside the farm market and dragged her inside. Deacon put a finger to his lips, silencing her once she realized it was him.

"On second thought," he said, "I never was any good at waiting to open presents."

He kissed her hard as he backed her up against a counter and released her to flip her over. She let out a little shriek, briefly startled. His hands were up her skirt, skimming over her lace panties and dragging them down.

"We're going to be late," she protested weakly as she stepped out of them.

Deacon grinned devilishly at her in the mirror behind the cash register. He shoved her panties in his pocket and tore open a condom with his teeth. Their eyes locked. Amaira's breath hitched.

"We'll save the slow stuff for later," he promised. "Right now, I plan to take you rough, and hard."

Amaira gulped, as passion ragged through her. An entire afternoon of teasing had her more than ready for him.

"Do it," she urged. "Do it now, Deacon."

Without another word, he slammed into her from behind. The counter rocked with the force of their bodies as they collided. Their eyes remained locked in the mirror as he pounded into her, over and over. Harder and harder. She didn't think she could take much more.

"Amaira," he ground out as he came.

The sound of his voice, thick with passion, was her undoing. Amaira bit her lip, trembling and clenching around his length as she came. Her knees weak, she collapsed on the wooden counter as Deacon withdrew from her body. Dimly she heard the snap of the condom as he pulled it off. She didn't know what he did with it, and she was too sated to care. He pulled her skirt down over her hips, and she forced herself to stand, using the mirror to tidy herself as best she could.

"I need my panties back please," she held out her hand to him and grinned smugly.

"Not a chance," he replied. "This is your punishment for keeping secrets from me."

"I thought this was my punishment," she gestured around the small building, and he laughed.

"This was merely a taste of my birthday gift," he said. "Your punishment is to go to this party without your sexy black panties, wondering when I might try for another taste."

Amaira protested, but he only laughed as he escorted her back outside. His "punishment" was cruel... but it secretly excited her as well, knowing they had this secret between them.

Chapter 17

"I love the silence of the country at night." – Travis's journal.

The night air was filled with the sound of crickets chirping in the fields, and gravel crunching beneath their feet as they made their way to the dark barn. Deacon glanced around, and except for a few extra tire tracks, would never have guessed there was a barn full of people waiting to jump out at him in a few moments. His family did a decent job concealing the party. If it weren't for the fact that no one had so much as called to wish him happy birthday, he would never have guessed there was a party in the works. He wondered who was going to be in that barn to surprise him, since he'd been overseas for years, he'd lost touch with most of his friends. Deacon glanced over at Amaira and grinned, slipping an arm around her waist to pull her closer.

"Thank you," he whispered as he kissed her cheek, letting the scent of her vanilla shampoo fill his senses.

"For what?" She asked softly. "For letting you seduce me in your family's store?"

"Well, there's that... but seriously, thank you for everything," he replied. "For being exactly what I've needed since I came home. For being willing to put up with my family's whims. For being you."

"Oh," she breathed. Before she could utter another word, Deacons lips descended on hers with all the tenderness that filled his heart.

"Damn the party," he whispered gruffly as he trailed his lips along her jaw. "All I want for my birthday is you. Come back to the house with me."

"Deacon, no. Your family put a lot of time and effort into this party. There will be plenty of time for the rest of your plans later. I promise," Amaira sighed as she reluctantly pushed him away and took a step back.

Deacon groaned, running his suddenly empty hands through his hair before adjusting himself and fixing his pants. She was right, but he still hated that she wasn't in his arms, his earlier excitement diminished as the hours stretched out ahead of them like a never-ending highway, or a clock with no hour hand that only ticks away the minutes. Tapping his fingers against his leg, he started walking towards the barn, struggling not to reach out and grab Amaira's hand and pull her close. As if she understood, Amaira kept pace with him, quickly fixing her smudged lipstick using her cellphone camera and a napkin she'd had tucked away in her clutch.

Pausing outside the large barn door, Deacon grasped the cold metal handle in his grasp and yanked. The door slid open with a screech and the creaking of wood to reveal an inky blackness inside. Anxiety ratcheted up his spine as he unexpectedly remembered the dark sewer, he never thought he'd escape. He squeezed his eyes closed fighting back the memories that threatened to overwhelm his senses. He was home, he reminded himself, walking into the barn he'd spent countless hours in growing up. His leg ached and sweat beaded his brow as he stood frozen to the spot, his trigger finger itching for his weapon while he continued to remind himself that his ordeal was far behind him now. He was home, and he was never going back overseas unless necessary, and not to the middle east. He reiterated it to himself like a mantra, trying to calm his sudden anxiety. Amaira, as if sensing his unease, frowned and strode past him into the barn. Seconds later light flooded the room. Spots filled his vision, and people were jumping out from every direction shouting "surprise" and "happy birthday."

People swarmed him from everywhere, shaking his hand and hugging him, oblivious to his internal struggles. Somehow, he managed to keep a neutral expression pasted on his face as he people he hadn't seen or spoken to in years wished him all the best. Amaira disappeared in the crowd with his sisters, who claimed to need her for a fashion emergency. Music started to play, and Deacon jerked, as if waking from a nightmare. He instantly recognized the song as one he'd written a lifetime ago. Someone thrusted a can of his mom's hard cider in his hands, and he eagerly popped the top to take a sip, savouring the tart apple and cinnamon flavours. Glancing around, he spotted his old band on a makeshift stage on the far side of the room and made his way over to them. His mom really had pulled out all the stops, he realized. Deacon was certain that most of these guys had long ago moved on to play with other bands. How had she managed to wrangle them together and drag them back here for a birthday party?

"Maybe we'll get to hear you play tonight? Like you did back in the old days?" A soft, feminine voice asked from somewhere off to his right.

"I doubt I still remember how to play," he replied turning, his smile freezing on his face, replaced with a look of astonishment. "Betty? What are you doing here? You look great!"

"Hey there GI Joe, welcome back! Oh, and happy birthday!" Betty exclaimed; her mass of brown curls tied back with an elastic that barely encompassed her thick hair. She looked like a pinup girl from the 1950's with her tight black leggings and white blouse with polka dots, a wide red belt emphasizing the look and her hourglass figure. Deacon raised a brow at the GI Joe comment and grinned.

"You still dating Charlie?" He asked, referring to his former best friend and lead guitarist currently lighting up the stage with his riffs. Before he'd joined the military, Betty had been a regular in their small audience during rehearsals, hanging out with the band as she sketched them. He'd teased her about her crush on Charlie, and she'd returned the favour by teasing him for his jealousy that Charlie was better looking. It had become a game to them, and then she'd made her move and finally asked Charlie out. The welcome memories helped push away his earlier distress.

"Nope. Finally made an honest man out of him," she grinned and held up her ring finger, brandishing the sapphire and diamond engagement ring and matching wedding band that adorned it.

"Well damn," Deacon exclaimed feeling Amaira sidle up next to him. "Wish I'd been there to watch the man take the plunge. Betty this is Amaira."

"Girlfriend?" Betty asked, holding out a hand to Amaira in greeting.

"I hope so or we've been having far too much fun in the bedroom," Amaira replied smoothly taking Betty's hand and shaking it. Betty chuckled.

"I was trying to get your man up on stage to play a set with the old band, but he's being all shy and nothing like the cocky bastard I remember," Betty elbowed Deacon in the gut.

"Things change. Like I said, I haven't picked up a guitar in years. Probably don't even remember how to play," Deacon replied.

"It's like riding a bike," Charlie was a big guy covered in tattoos, his hair slicked back to show off his piercings.

He held out a guitar to Deacon as he nodded at the stage where the rest of the band continued to play. Deacon sucked in a harsh breath, instantly recognizing the smooth lines and glossy white embossing. He hadn't seen it since the night Layla had claimed to have slept with his stepfather and threatened to destroy his family.

"Is that…?" He started to ask, despite the instant recognition. Alex and his mother had given him the Gibson for his fifteenth birthday. It was Alex who'd placed his first guitar in his hands and taught him to play. There were so many memories wrapped up in the wood and strings, and he kicked himself for leaving it behind.

"I held on to her for you while you were gone. Figured you might want her back one day," Charlie shrugged nonchalantly. "Least you could do is play a set with us. For old time's sake."

"Damn…. I don't know…." Deacon stared at the guitar reverently, carefully taking it from Charlie's hands and played a few notes. His instrument was perfectly tuned, and Deacon found that his fingers were itching to play it. He nodded and Charlie clapped him on the shoulder. Betty and Amaira cheered and soon everyone joined in as he stepped foot on stage. Deacon shook hands with his former bandmates, and the lead singer, Karl, who'd apparently replaced him when he left. Karl raised an irritated brow, his chains jangling as he crossed his scrawny arms.

"Don't think this means you get to resume your place here," Karl muttered with a barely suppressed snarl as he clapped Deacon on the shoulder. "Happy birthday."

"Thanks for keeping my spot warm," Deacon replied with a smirk. He could hear Charlie chuckle from somewhere nearby, but he didn't dare take his eyes off the man in front of him as they stared each other down. "But I'm going to be needing it back now. At least for tonight, so please, feel free to hit the bar for some refreshment."

Karl took a step towards him, and Charlie stepped between them. He said something so low, Deacon couldn't catch a single word, but the expression on Charlie's face spoke volumes. Even after all these years away, Deacon could still read him like an open book. Charlie was pissed and had no love for his lead singer. Karl pasted a smile on his face and stepped off the stage, stalking out of the barn.

"Sorry bout that," Charlie turned and gestured towards the restless crowd. "Still think you got it in you to entertain these fine folks?"

Deacon grinned.

"Let's find out," he replied. "Still remember how to play 'Born of Fire?'"

"Let's find out," Charlie repeated with a smirk as he grabbed his guitar and took his place next to Deacon.

"Evening folks," Deacon turned to the crowd and spoke into the microphone. He took a deep breath, but he wasn't nervous at all. The stage was his second home and being on it was as natural to him as breathing. "It's been a while since I've played but here's hoping I haven't forgotten how. Thank you all for coming out to celebrate my birthday tonight. I know you probably had better things to do than listen to me butcher this song, so the next round is on me."

"It's an open bar!" Someone shouted from the back and Deacon chuckled. He glanced at Amaira, smiling up at him from the front row, and slid the guitar strap over his head. His fingers danced over the strings, and the guitar sang. Deacon closed his eyes, relief and joy filling his body as the music washed over him. It might have been years since he'd played, but he hadn't forgotten how and standing here with his old band backing him up, it was the best homecoming he could have wished for. Deacon stepped closer to the microphone as Charlie and the rest of the band joined in playing the song. Amaira cheered and clapped, his sisters joining her in front of the small stage. He opened his mouth and let the lyrics to Born of Fire pour from his lips.

"Hair like fire,

She takes after her sire.

Heart in flames,

She hates the fame,

But

She's born of fire."

He almost missed Layla stepping into the barn, a blond-haired little girl in a pink dress and matching headband in her hair following timidly behind her.

111

Chapter 18

"I went on a double date with Trevor and his wife last night. It was a blind date, and the first I'd been on since Rose passed away a year ago. The woman was perfectly nice, but I wasn't attracted to her at all. The entire date was awkward as hell, trying to find things to talk about. Maybe I'm not ready to move on after all." -Travis's journal

Amaira danced with Tana, laughing, and having a blast as Deacon played like he was born with a guitar in his hand. He had more presence on stage than the lead singers for the last five concerts she'd seen, and he was doing it in a barn decorated with strings of lights, balloons, and streamers. It was incredible. How on Earth could he let a bitch like Layla derail his music career? He was a natural. Listening to the lyrics of his song, it was easy to tell he'd written it for his mom. Born of Fire… she liked it. It would make a great title for her script, she realized and decided to mention it to Deacon… tomorrow. Tonight, was about him.

Spinning, she almost tripped over her feet, saved only by the quick reflexes of a tall man whose dimples accented his smile when he turned it on her. She started to apologize and froze mid sentence when she noticed Deacon's ex walk in with a little girl who looked as if she wished to be anywhere else. Layla had a sour expression on her face as she took in the crowd raving and dancing, her eyes fixed on the man lighting up the stage with his guitar. She tossed her hair and roughly grabbed the little girl by the arm, practically dragging her as she shoved her way to the front of the stage. Amaira's heart sank at the tortured expression on the child's face.

"What is *she* doing here?" Tana demanded, coming to Amaira's side. Amaira tried to tear her eyes away from the scene unfolding before her, but it was like watching a train crash in slow motion. She simply couldn't move as Layla stepped up on the stage and practically shoved Charlie out the way. Betty yelled and started to storm the stage but froze at the slight shake of Charlie's head. The music stopped abruptly, and the barn descended into chaos as dancers tripped over each other and everyone's attention turned to the woman on stage.

"I can't believe that bitch had the nerve to drag that poor child into this mess. How dare she?" Amy muttered, appearing behind them, and shaking Amaira free of her shock.

How could someone stoop so low? Stealing her spine, Amaira shoved her way through the crowd and barely made it through the small crowd forming between her and Deacon. She couldn't let Layla do this to him. She couldn't let her ruin Deacon's birthday, and his life, anymore than she already had. Before she could reach the stage, however, Layla's perfect lips parted and her voice rang through the barn, echoing in the rafters.

"Good evening, everyone. Some of you may remember me, I'm Deacon's ex-girlfriend Layla for those of you that don't. Anyway, Deacon dearest, YOUR DAUGHTER AND I WANTED TO WISH YOU HAPPY BIRTHDAY." Layla spat out the words like a foul venom that poisoned the entire party.

"What?!" Tana and Amy shouted in unison.

Amaira watched as Deacon's eyes moved from Layla to the little girl, moving from them to search the crowd. She followed his eyes as they locked on his mother's shocked expression, his

113

face hardening as he tore his gaze away and fixated on the ground beneath his feet. She swallowed, wishing there was something she could do to make this better. Her heart ached with the knowledge that there was nothing that she or anyone, but Deacon, could do. He cleared his throat, opening his mouth and shutting it before he finally spoke, his face grim as he nodded to himself. She hoped he would publicly denounce her the way Layla deserved.

"Thank you, Layla and Sonia. Enjoy the rest of the party everyone," he somehow managed to keep his voice steady as he spoke. Amaira shut her eyes, a single tear escaping down her cheek as she tried to gulp in air. She couldn't believe he would let that woman manipulate him again. Especially after he swore, he would never let Layla sink her claws into him anymore. Her sorrow grew into fury, igniting the blood in her veins until she feared she would burst into flames.

Deacon handed off his guitar and stormed off the stage, the crowd parting before him like the Red Sea. Amaira followed close behind him as he ignored his swarming family and their buzz of questions. He froze in front of his mother, unable to meet her gaze. Her eyes were full of unspoken questions, her body tense. Deacon gulped, then turned and fled the party.

"Why did you let her get away with that?" Amaira demanded, furiously stalking behind him through the shelter of the orchard. "How on Earth could you let her publicly claim you as the father of her child, without a word of defense? She made you look like a deadbeat in there! A deadbeat dad who didn't even tell his family of his daughter's existence. You have to tell them the truth, Deacon!"

"You wouldn't understand!" Deacon barked, surprising her.

"Explain it to me then! You told me you were done letting that bitch manipulate you by threatening your family, and yet you're still letting her do it!" She wanted to scream. "Do you still have feelings for her?"

"Amaira." Deacon paused. "How could you even ask me that? You know I don't."

"Why shouldn't I ask you that, Deacon? Because it looks to me as if you're still letting her control your life! Why would you do that if you didn't care for her?" She crossed her arms protectively over her chest, the need to hear his answer at war with the fear that coursed through her that it wouldn't be what she hoped.

"You don't.... You know what? Go back to the party. Or better yet, go home. You've got your story now. There's nothing left for you here." He quietly commanded then disappeared into the night, leaving Amaira gaping after him, her heart breaking in the solitude of the night as the wind dried her tears. He was gone.

She stood there staring at the empty row of trees, disbelief and shock changing to anger and hurt. The barn was still lit up, and she could hear music playing as the band tried to get the party restarted, but Amaira couldn't bring herself to return to the party. Instead, she kicked off her heels and scooped them up before fleeing to her rental car. Remembering that her keys were in the house, she quickly changed direction, stormed up the front steps and inside the house, and raced to her room. She grabbed her suitcase and tossed her belongings inside, desperate to be gone before he returned. If this is what it means to love, she decided she didn't want it after all. The pain in her chest was too much for her to bear. She'd drown in it. Once she'd finished packing, she closed the luggage, grabbed the handle and her keys off the dresser and let the door close behind her with a final, resounding click.

Chapter 19

"Regret is a powerful thing. There are so many things I regret in my life. But I refuse to let them drag me down. I could drown in a sea of regret if I let myself wallow in it. Instead, I vow to live my life as best I can. I refuse to let anyone take my happiness from me anymore. Not even a ghost from the past." -Travis's journal

Deacon grabbed a rock off the beach and skipped it across the inky black lake. The stone caused ripples to spread further and further across the otherwise still water until they disappeared. To his left, the bright lights of the Toronto skyline lit up the horizon, but here it was completely dark and exactly what he needed. He didn't want his problems to be lit up for the entire world to see, exposed like a wound on his soul. The rustle of leaves behind him, and the snap of a twig told him he wasn't alone, but he didn't bother turning around. He picked up another rock and tossed it.

"Are you alright?" His mother asked. "I told Layla to leave."

"I'm fine," Deacon replied after a few minutes, his voice breaking slightly as he spoke.

"You're lying," Sarah replied. "I can tell. We don't have to talk about it if you don't want to, but I'd like to sit here with you, if that's ok?"

Deacon nodded jerkily, reluctantly grateful for her presence. It tore him apart inside, knowing that the truth might shatter her, and he wracked his brain for explanations. But the only thing he could decide on was the truth. His own words echoed through his brain as he remembered the lyrics of the song that he'd written for her when he was kid. She really was stronger than he gave her credit for. He'd had no idea, until this moment, just how strong though, and took a deep shuddering breath. If anyone would understand… it would be his mom. Shuffling his feet, he moved to sit next to her, resting his head on her shoulder like he had when he was a child. Sarah wrapped her arms around him and held him as close as she could given his larger size, pressing a kiss to the top of his head. She didn't say a word, simply sat there and held him without judgement, and it was exactly what he'd needed, he was surprised to realize. He might be thirty years old, but in that moment, he felt like that little twelve-year-old boy whose family had been torn apart by an unfaithful father figure all over again.

"Mom?" he whispered quietly. "Has Alex ever… ever cheated on you?"

"Alex? No, never. Why? Did Layla do that to you?" She squeezed his shoulder sympathetically. "Oh honey, I'm so sorry. No wonder you left so abruptly after you broke up with her."

"It's more than that, Mom." Deacon sucked in a deep breath, shutting his eyes briefly. "She uh… she cheated with someone, and that man got her pregnant. She claimed the baby was mine, but the dates didn't match up. I'd been away on tour for too long for it to even be a possibility. She kept insisting that the baby was mine though, and no matter how much I cared for her, I couldn't stop thinking about Bruce. Bruce might have raised me like I was his own but knowing that I wasn't his son nearly destroyed him. It destroyed our family. Don't get me wrong, I'm glad that Jack's my father and not Bruce, but I can't help wondering how different our lives might have been if he had been my real father. If he might have treated us differently."

"Oh sweetheart! Bruce was always a bit rough around the edges. I never should have married him; I was a foolish girl back then. I'm so sorry I did that to you. You must think I'm the worst mother," she choked back a sob.

"No, I don't. That's just it. I get why you did it. You wanted someone to love you, and when my dad left, you thought Bruce was that man. How could you have known that Jack had gotten you pregnant or that Bruce wasn't my father? The timing… it was so much closer than the timing of my being with Layla and her announcing the pregnancy, I can see how you made that mistake. I cared so much for Layla, but I didn't love her and when I found out she'd cheated… it didn't destroy me the same way it destroyed Bruce. I knew a DNA test would prove it in court if I had to go that route."

"Why did you never tell anyone about this?" She asked, quietly stroking his hair as she tightened her hold on him. "I would have helped you."

"I know and I wanted to tell you so many times. But then Layla demanded that I pay her child support, or she'd reveal the identity of her child's paternity. I couldn't bear to look at her or hear her voice as she introduced me as Sonia's father, so I did the most rational thing I could think of at the time," he explained. "I left."

"Joining the army to get away from your extortionist ex-girlfriend was rational?" His mother asked, her voice dripping with skepticism and scorn. "I don't understand why you thought it rational to let her claim that child as yours in the first place."

"Now that I think about it… maybe not so much," Deacon chuckled, quickly sobering again as he continued his story. "The thing is… she claimed the baby's father was…."

"Alex?" Sarah guessed shrewdly and Deacon bolted upright, staring at her with a million questions all trying to spill out of his mouth at once.

"She wouldn't be the first to try and make that claim," Sarah sighed, surprising him. Had his stepfather cheated on his mother after all? His blood started to boil, and his hand tightened into a fist. "But living with Bruce all those years taught me how to spot

119

a liar and a cheater a mile away. Alex has NEVER and would never cheat on me. It's funny… DNA and lawyers are a great deterrent against liars. And he's always been careful never to hurt me like Bruce did. They might both be charming and handsome, but Alex doesn't have a deceptive bone in his body. I promise you he's never cheated on me! And he would never have laid a hand on Layla! That girl has a lot of nerve manipulating you like that! Oh, my sweet, sweet boy. I can't believe you've born that all these years without a single word to anyone. No wonder you rarely ever came home."

"I'm so sorry mom," Deacon cried. "I was scared that her accusations would shatter you again, and it would destroy Amy and Riley and… and…."

"Shh…. It's ok, Deacon. I'm ok. I'm not the shell of a woman I was when I divorced Bruce. If anything, my ability to love and trust a man like Alex with my heart, after Bruce's infidelities and abuse… it should show you how strong I am. And you are strong too. We're Mackenzie's after all. Our name literally means born of fire, and we'll get through this. Together. No more secrets," she said.

Deacon sighed, shutting his eyes as the breeze from the lake washed over him as if washing away the years of hurt and anger. Talking with his mother, his heart was suddenly lighter, and he'd wished he'd done this sooner. The chip on his shoulder that had weighed his every decision for the past ten years was completely gone.

"What I'd really like to know however, is who is that poor girl's real father?" Sarah asked, her brow wrinkling with concentration as she stared out at the lake, the light of the moon reflecting off its surface. Deacon frowned. As much as he wanted to be rid of Layla, he would never forgive himself if he hurt that poor innocent child. An innocent child that believed he was her father… and probably grew up believing that he didn't care about her. The idea sent a dagger through his heart, forcing him to gasp from the pain. Pain he had inadvertently caused in avoiding a confrontation with Layla and her schemes.

"Mom?" He choked. "Sonia's grown up believing I was her father. She's going to be devastated. Haven't I hurt her enough by refusing to acknowledge her? As much as I love Jack… it hurt like hell to find out that he was my real father and he'd wanted nothing to do with me when I was a child. It still hurts sometimes. How can I do that to someone else?"

"Oh Honey! Jack staying away for all those years had nothing to do with you, and everything to do with me. It wasn't your fault. I was broken when he left. If I had waited for him… if I hadn't eloped with Bruce… who knows what might have happened. Nothing I say or do will ever make it up to you. I can never apologize enough for all the hurt and anger I caused you. But we can't live our lives with what if's haunting our future. We can't do anything to fix the past, but we can do something about the here and now. Whatever you decide to do, know that your entire family supports you."

"What if I decide to claim Sonia as my own? What if I let Layla win?" He asked softly, staring intently at his hands as they clenched and unclenched in his lap. His mother turned and placed her hand on his, pausing his movements and forcing him to look up at her. Her eyes glistened with tears, and her face was pinched with sorrow.

"Then, as that little girl's grandmother, I have to ask you if you honestly believe that living with her mother is the best place for her to be. She deserves a father who will not let her mother continue to manipulate the lives of everyone around her. Sonia deserves to have a normal childhood. Can you give her that?"

"Yeah, I think I can," he said, his voice hoarse and thick with emotion.

His mother's smile was full of sorrow and pride as she leaned over to embrace him again, holding him tight as if afraid to let him go. Deacon had no idea how long they sat like that, hugging each other, before Sarah broke the silence surrounding them.

"You are so much like my father," she whispered tearfully. "After my mother died, he did everything he could to make sure I grew up having as much of a normal childhood as he could possibly provide."

"You're mother…?" Deacon asked, confused as he pulled away. He knew his grandmother had died in a car accident when his mom was a little girl, but he'd never dreamed that she knew that truth as well. Especially since his grandfather had done everything, he possibly could, to hide it from her.

"I know he told us that she divorced him and abandoned us. I found his journal after he passed away, and I'm positive you've seen it too, so don't pretend you don't know what I'm talking about," she gently admonished, dashing her tears away with the back of her hand. "I was hurt at first, but I understand why he did it. He was so strong! I never gave him enough credit while he was alive, for everything he'd been through and everything my mother and I put him through. When I look at you, I see that same strength. You might be torn now, but you always seem to do what is right, no matter how hard it may be. This little girl might believe you're her father, but remember, somewhere out there, there's a man who really is. What if he doesn't know about her and could give her everything she deserves. Could you live with that knowledge? Whatever you decide, I'm here for you Deacon. Always. But I have one request."

"What is it?" Deacon asked, his brows pinching together.

"Stop keeping secrets from me because you're afraid I can't handle it. I'm stronger than you and my father give me credit for," she admonished. "You're not the only Mackenzie's that were born with fire in their veins."

122

Deacon chuckled, surprised and agreed.

Chapter 20

"Am I destined to be alone? I honestly believed Rose was my soulmate. Does that mean there is no one else out there for me? Or do we have another soulmate? Or was she not my soulmate and my true soulmate is still out there somewhere? Are second chances real? I don't know, but my brain keeps asking all these questions every time I try to shut my eyes.

The Henderson's are talking about moving south to be with their family. Maybe our neighbours will sell their farm to me. An expansion might be the perfect distraction from my rambling thoughts and aching heart. Busy hands and all that." - Travis's journal

Amaira jerked awake. Disoriented, her heart pounded as she stared at the dark ceiling of her bedroom. After being away for so long, she'd started to forget what it looked like. Her heart twinged as she remembered why she was home again so soon, and she fought back the tears that pooled at the corners of her eyes. Sitting up, she groggily searched for the source of the annoyingly piercing sound that had woken her. Finding her cellphone buried under the rumpled dress she'd discarded the moment she'd stepped foot inside her apartment in the middle of the night, she glanced at the time. Eight in the morning, California time. She did the quick time zone calculation and realized she'd been home barely four hours. After a long day shopping with Deacon, and an even longer night at the airport waiting for a flight, it was no wonder she was exhausted. She hadn't slept a wink on the plane either, constantly replaying their fight in her mind over and over again. There was only one person who would be calling her so early. One person whom she'd bothered to text when her plane landed at LAX.

"Hi Mom," she answered groggily, putting the phone on speaker as she slouched into the kitchen and searched her bare cupboards, hoping to find some small bit of coffee.

"What happened? Why am I getting mysterious text messages in the middle of the night with a simple 'I'm home?' No explanation, no notice. We weren't expecting you for a couple weeks. What is going on Amaira?" Vivienne's Brooklyn accent thickened with concern, dropping the posh accent she'd adopted during her career.

Amaira groaned and mimicked banging her head on the cupboards. Her father would have at least let her sleep a few extra hours before grilling her. She should have known better, but she'd been too exhausted, to think clearly when she'd landed.

"Nothing happened," she lied. She wasn't ready to go into all the details without a giant mug of java in her veins. "I missed being home and decided I'd spent enough time at the farm around Xander and his family to write the script. He wants to see something be the end of next week and I thought it might be easier to concentrate here. That's all."

"So, you hopped on a plane in the middle of the night without telling anyone? I know you better than that, Amaira. Don't lie to me," her mother commanded. Amaira could hear her mother's irritation dripping through the phone line. "What happened?"

"Mom, I'm fine. Let's meet for dinner at that bistro you like, ok? I'll tell you everything then. Right now, I need an epic boost of caffeine and my kitchen's collecting dust. I see tumble weeds blowing across the pantry. It's a complete disaster in here. I'll see you at seven!" She ended the call and groaned. There was no coffee anywhere in this empty nest.

~~~

An hour later, Amaira emerged from her apartment, refreshed from a hot shower and starving. Fortunately, there was a small bodega a short walk from her apartment, and a Starbucks on the way. She took a deep breath of the familiar Los Angeles air, savouring it for a moment before joining the crowds of pedestrians hurrying to their various destinations. She refused to compare her life in the city with the life she'd experienced on the farm.

The door chimed as she walked inside the cafe, the air buzzing with conversation and the scent of fresh ground coffee beans. She ordered a latte and biscotti to go and moved aside to wait for her order once she'd paid. It was all so mundane and ordinary, exactly what she needed. Not a single drop of lust, love, or drama. The barista grinned as he handed her a large cup of coffee and a paper bag. She barely suppressed a groan when she noticed a phone number written on the sleeve of the cup. She forced herself to smile at the man behind the counter with his long hair piled in a man-bun on the top of his head, and deep brown eyes. He was cute, but his smile did nothing for her. Not a single tremor in the pit of her stomach. She thanked him and left, devouring the biscotti the rest of the way to the bodega. Her cupboards were woefully bare, and now that she'd scrubbed the dust from every inch of them, she desperately needed to fill them before she decided to binge on fast food and drown her sorrows with empty calories. She refused to be one of those heartbroken women who let their stomachs dictate their emotions.

Once she was home, her groceries tucked away, Amaira slumped down the wall and cried. Her anger had completely evaporated, and her chest squeezed as if gripped in a vise. She couldn't breathe, except to drag in short gasps of air between sobs. How could he do this to her? How could one man have this effect on her heart? She didn't understand any of it, and wished she'd never met Deacon Mackenzie. Eventually her tears subsided, and she crawled over to her couch, turned on the tv to her favourite daytime talk show and passed out, emotionally exhausted and oblivious to her phone ringing where she'd left it on the kitchen counter.

Chapter 21

"It's hard to trust someone with your heart. I used to think it was fragile and delicate. But it's not. It's strong this heart of mine, and I see it in my daughter too. I worry she might take after her mother, that she might be taken from me someday to join her where I wouldn't be able to follow. But she's not. Sarah's heart is like mine. The Mackenzie heart is strong. There's a fire that burns in our veins, and every trial only makes it stronger." - Travis's journal

Deacon wasn't surprised to find that Amaira had done what he'd asked and left. What he hadn't expected was for her to do it in the middle of the night. He sat on the foot of her bed, his head in his hands and groaned. He had no right talking to her like that, but he wasn't in the right frame of mind at the time. With all the drama with Layla and his family, she didn't deserve to be dragged into any of that. As much as it hurt, she was probably better off without him. He couldn't do anything to fix what he'd said and done, but he could do something about the little girl that called him dad. He hadn't stayed up all night with his mom working on a plan to either get Layla to admit her extortion or gain custody of Sonia for nothing. They agreed that the little girl deserved better and were determined to do what they could to give that to her. If he was going to be a dad, he decided he'd better start acting like it and grow up. The first thing he was going to do was stop wallowing in self pity and call Amaira to make sure she at least got home safely. Grabbing his phone, he left Amaira's room and dialed the number she'd given him. Unsure of what he would say, he paced anxiously, the floorboards creaking beneath his feet, waiting as the phone rang and rang, only to get her voicemail.

"Hey, it's… uh… it's Deacon. I wanted to apologize for the things I said, and I hope you got home alright. I'm assuming that's where you went when you left last night anyway. I'll understand if you don't call me back, but I hope you do," he ended the call, pressing his eyes closed and fighting the urge to hop on a plane to California. She was right, he did deserve better than Layla, but Amaira deserved so much more than him. If she didn't return his call, he'd simply have to accept that she wanted nothing to do with him. He deserved that. So long as she was safe and happy, he supposed that was all he could really hope for. Pushing off the wall, he stalked downstairs to grab a bite to eat before hitting the field for a jog while he inspected the perimeter of the orchard for signs of deer.

Outside, he paused next to the barn, and detoured inside. Charlie had left his guitar, propped on a stand in the middle of the small stage. Drawn to it, Deacon picked it up and strummed a couple chords. The sound reverberated through the room and his body, igniting his blood with the same familiar fire he'd believed had long ago burnt to ash. Perhaps, if he couldn't have the woman he loved, he could at least have this back. Music. His first true love. His inspection duties forgotten, he hit record on his phone, tossed the strap over his shoulder and started singing while he played. His pain pouring out of his guitar.

<hr />

Flowers in hand, Deacon locked his truck and crossed the quiet street towards the small, tidy yellow bungalow with a rusty blue Honda civic in the driveway. Layla would probably kill him if she knew he was here, but he couldn't care less. Raising his

129

fist, he gave the screen door a quick knock that reverberated through the house and yard. A child's laughter danced in the air as the door swung open. Sonia stood there, frozen in her denim shorts and purple butterfly shirt, her blond hair in pig tails that rested on her shoulders. A frail, elderly woman with a scarf covering her hair and framing her pale face stood behind the little girl. Deacon instantly recognized her, surprised by the drastic changes in her appearance since they'd last spoken. She had a look of resignation in her eyes as she recognized him in return.

"I heard you were back. Might as well come in," she held the door open and invited him inside the home where Layla had grown up. It was sparsely decorated with furniture that belonged in a museum, and photographs everywhere of Layla and her sisters through the years, and of Sonia as a baby and various school functions. He wanted to dive into all those pictures of the little girl with her big blue eyes and experience those memories he'd done everything he could to avoid. A pang of guilt stabbed through him, and he forced himself to follow Layla's mother through the small living room and into the tiny kitchen, taking a seat across from her at the table.

"Sonia, the kettle please," she instructed, gesturing to the electric kettle resting on the counter next to the sink. Sonia rushed to do as her grandmother asked and filled the kettle and plugged it in.

"Thank you dear. Why don't you go outside and play now for a bit while the grown-ups chat?" Sonia glanced shyly at him and then turned and dashed out the kitchen door and into the backyard. He watched her climb into a tire swing hanging from a giant oak tree in the backyard with a book in her hand. She opened the book, but glared back at him instead, her book forgotten on her lap. Hurt and anger were clearly written all over her face.

"Sonia told me what my daughter did last night at your party," Selena's voice dragged Deacon's attention away from the window. "I'm sorry about that. I don't know where I went so wrong with her! Her sisters are married, with degrees and successful careers of their own. But Layla, she's...."

"You don't have to apologize for her," Deacon replied honestly. "I'm not here about Layla... well actually I guess I am. I don't want to be a prick, but I know I'm not Sonia's biological father. I was away on tour when Layla got pregnant, but I couldn't deal with the news like I should have back then and I'm sorry. I plan on claiming Sonia as my own, but before I file custody papers, I need to know one thing first."

Selena wrung her frail, delicate hands, her eyes glancing everywhere around the room, before finally coming to rest on the flowers he'd placed on the table.

"Are those for me?" She nodded at the bundle of daisies. Deacon had completely forgotten about them.

"Sorry, I meant to give them to you sooner," he replied sheepishly, passing the flowers across the table. Selena stood and moved towards the sink, searching the cupboard beneath it until she pulled out a vase and filled it with water. She set to work arranging the flowers in the vase and placing them on the counter, before making a pot of tea. She placed a mug in front of him with a sugar bowl and a small pitcher of milk.

"Are you hungry?" She asked, opening the cupboard, but Deacon stopped her before she could pile food on the table in front of him. He knew she was trying to avoid his questions, but he couldn't leave without the answers he was looking for and he

131

knew he'd never get them from Layla. If anyone could answer his questions, it would be her mother. He rose from his chair, and gently closed the cupboard.

"I'm sorry, Selena, but I really need to know. Who is Sonia's real father and why isn't he here instead of me?" He quietly asked. Layla's mother sighed, sinking back into her chair.

"It's not really my secret to share, but I don't have forever to wait for Layla to become a better person and own up to her mistakes. That girl is as stubborn as her father, you understand. She loved you so much, and I think that's why she refuses to let go. Unfortunately, she's using Sonia to hold on to you anyway she can. It's honorable of you not to call her out the way she deserves, but you have already been through so much and it's not fair to you or Sonia or her real father to let Layla keep doing this. It isn't fair. It's not right!" Selena sighed, dropping her head into her hands. "Sonia's father is a man named Nate Thompson. He's a mechanic down at that shop on First Street. He's a good man, but he doesn't have the money and connections that you do. He can't afford to take Layla to court, so he comes by to visit with Sonia whenever her mother isn't around. He's afraid if Layla knew, she'd take Sonia and skip town or do something that would keep him from her."

"Like publicly announcing that someone else is Sonia's father," Deacon ironically pointed out. Selena smiled sadly at him before continuing.

"He doesn't make as much as he could if he left town, but he refuses to leave Sonia behind and he can't afford a lawyer to fight for his rights as her father." She wrung her hands and turned her attention to the little girl now quietly reading in her swing. "What are you going to do?"

Deacon grinned, feeling a million times lighter than he had since the day Layla had blackmailed him into supporting her and her daughter. A new plan began to form, and he was eager to put it in motion.

"I'm going to help a father reunite with his daughter, if that's what he truly wants" he replied. "And I believe my truck is overdue for an oil change. Oh, and one more thing. How much of this does Sonia know?"

"That girl is very bright, and she has a big heart. She doesn't deserve to be lied to," Selena replied honestly and that was all the answer Deacon needed. He smiled and bid her farewell, his tea untouched as he rose from the table and saw himself out.

Chapter 22

"Sometimes I dream of Rose. The scent of her skin, or the warmth of her body. The sound of her laughter. The dreams are becoming fainter with every day that passes. It's becoming easier to breathe, but it doesn't mean I miss her any less. It would be easier if she had left me to live her life somewhere out in the world, the way I told our daughter she had. I believed it was a kindness I couldn't give myself at first, but sometimes I wonder if it wasn't worse. To believe that she is out there somewhere, or to know that she has gone where I can't follow? Which is worse?"

-Travis's journal

The heat of his breath raised gooseflesh along her skin, causing her to shiver with excitement. She writhed beneath him, begging him to let go of her hands so she could touch him too. He simply grinned teasingly as his grip kept her arms above her head while he feasted on her body. She arched her back, pressing her body closer as he unbuttoned her shorts with his free hand and slipped it inside. His lips trailed along her throat and collarbone as his fingers found her mound and drew lazy circles that had her calling his name and begging for more. Deacon knew exactly what she wanted and how to touch her to drive her mad with passion. She struggled against his grip, but he held her firmly as his hand moved from her body. Amaira whimpered from the loss of his touch, but it was soon replaced with the heat of his body. She didn't know what happened to her clothes, or where his had disappeared too, but she didn't care. She couldn't wait any longer. She needed to feel him moving inside her, his movements tightening the coil inside her that was beginning to unravel.

"Amaira," he whispered her name over and over as he plunged inside her. She gasped with excitement, her heart pounding so hard she feared it might burst from her chest.

"Amaira," he whispered urgently. "Open your eyes Amaira. Look at me."

She did as he bade her, and instantly regretted her decision as reality slammed into her. Laughter sounded in the background. She jumped and barely suppressed a scream before she realized she was in her own apartment, and it was her mother sitting on the chair next to her that had woken her, the television blasting a comedy show. She should have known he wouldn't be here with her. He'd dismissed her in the cruelest way. As if she didn't matter at all. The pain crashed over her like a tidal wave, and she struggled to contain it, wishing she could bury it deep inside where it wouldn't hurt anymore. But her mother was never going to let her do that, she realized. Vivienne was a firm believer in exercising inner demons and came prepared with a tub of her favourite gelato that was currently melting on her coffee table. Amaira grabbed the remote and clicked off the television with its distractingly loud laugh track.

"Mom," she said, a little breathlessly as she choked back her tears "What are you doing here? I thought we were meeting at the restaurant?"

"So did I, but when you didn't show, I decided to come check on you," her mom replied, standing gracefully as she moved to the kitchen and came back with two spoons. She popped off the lid of the gelato and sent it flying across the table in a way that made Amaira giggle. She glanced at the clock and realized that it had grown much later than she'd realized.

"I'm sorry mom. I planned to have a short nap, but I must have forgotten to set my alarm," she answered sheepishly as she took the spoon her mother offered to her.

"It's fine dear, but you should really have your phone nearby. I tried calling you a hundred times," she took a small delicate bite and let the flavours melt over her tongue as she savoured it.

"Now, tell me what happened. Do not spare any details. I want to know everything," her mother commanded and Amaira found herself opening up to her mother in a way she couldn't remember ever doing in the past when she'd broken up with a boyfriend. But no other man had ever made her feel the things that Deacon had, nor broken her heart as ruthlessly. By the time she'd finished her tale, Amaira realized glumly that she'd eaten the entire tub of gelato. Vivienne took the tub and her spoon and placed it back on the table, then reached over and wrapped Amaira in her warm embrace, stroking her hair in that soothing way she'd always done when Amaira had scraped her knee as a child or lost a gymnastics competition.

"It's alright, Amaira. Let it all out," she whispered as Amaira cried on her shoulder until she had exhausted herself again. "You are a strong, intelligent, beautiful woman, Amaira, and if he can't appreciate that, he doesn't deserve your heart. Leave him to his self-imposed prison and when you're ready, move on with your life. It might not feel like it now, but the pain will go away someday. Write that script and then forget all about him. Put all that emotion and heartache into it, and you'll have an Oscar worthy movie on your hands."

Amaira smiled through her tears. Her mother always seemed to know what to say. It was another reason she admired her so much. She'd never given her enough credit before.

136

"Thanks mom. Maybe you're right. I should let it all out and pour my heart and soul into this movie. It might prove cathartic. Writing has always done that for me." She admitted, staring longingly at the empty tub in front of her, and wishing it was a magically refilling one like she imagined they'd have at Hogwarts, and sighed.

Chapter 23

"There's this woman at Sarah's school. I believe she's a teacher there, but it's possible she's a parent. I'm drawn to her infectious laughter, hoping to hear the tinkle of her voice when she speaks. It's been so long since I've felt this way. Maybe there is hope for me after all...."

-Travis's journal

"What did you do to Amaira?" Amy demanded as she stormed through the back door, anger radiating from her in a way that reminded him of a Fury from Greek mythology. "You better not have hurt her, Deacon! Why did she leave in the middle of the night?"

"Stay out of it, Amy. My relationship with Amaira is none of your business," Deacon placed his cup in the kitchen sink. He purposely ignored his sister as she fumed behind him, her hands on the quartz countertop of the island that separated them. His heart squeezed with guilt, but he refused to discuss his relationships with his little sister.

"Is it because of Layla? You can't seriously be considering taking her back after all these years! I don't care if she had your kid! She doesn't deserve you!" Amy persisted.

Deacon ignored her as he washed up his breakfast dishes and dried his hands on a towel, desperately grasping the last straws of his patience as she continued berating him. He deserved it after all, so why should he get upset with her? "The last time you took up with Layla... it nearly cost you your life! Guess we know now why you suddenly left and joined the damn army without any explanation. What the hell were you thinking Deacon?!"

"Enough!" He roared, and instantly regretted it when he saw the hurt that crossed her face, but he'd lost the battle with keeping his patience in check. "Look, I'm sorry I yelled, but my relationships or lack thereof are none of your business so butt out and leave me be."

He strode past her and let the screen door slam closed behind him as he took off for a quick jog through the fields, hoping to burn off some of his frustration. He didn't have a clue what to do about Amaira. She still refused to answer his phone calls. At least he knew she was safe, since her last voicemail message changed from "Hey you know what to do," to "Eat shit Deacon!" He couldn't deny that he deserved it. He was tempted to hop on a flight to Los Angeles, but he had too many problems to deal with at home, and he had no idea what he would even say to her or how to find her. He couldn't fix things with Amaira, but there was one problem he could fix.

The used car dealership where Nate Thompson worked as a mechanic brought back old memories of Deacon's childhood. The cars packing the lot were different, but the building hadn't changed a bit. It was just his luck that the one man he needed to talk to, happened to work for the man that had claimed to be his father for the first twelve years of his life, and nearly destroyed his family. Bruce Kitsman had taken over the dealership after his uncle had retired when Deacon was in high school, but that was about all Deacon knew of his life after he'd learned that Jack was his real father. Bruce was an abusive prick to his mother for years, and Deacon hated him for it. But now he was beginning to understand him a little better. What kind of man would he have become if he'd let Layla walk all over him ten years ago when she'd announced her pregnancy? If he'd married her and claimed Sonia as his own? Would knowing she wasn't his, have slowly poisoned his soul? If Layla had left him and taken Sonia, told everyone the truth... could he have survived that kind of pain? If it hadn't been for his life with Bruce, he might not have walked away. Maybe it was worse knowing that Layla was deliberately using him, extorting money from him. This mess was partly his fault and he needed to do something to try and fix it. He hoped it wasn't a decade too late.

Stepping inside the small office, he was greeted by fake plants and a water cooler. A woman stood behind the desk, her brown hair pulled back in a ponytail and grease smudges on her face and overalls. She looked up at him as he stepped inside and gave him a friendly smile, the crows feet crinkling at the corners of her eyes.

"Welcome to Kitsman Auto. Are you shopping or fixing?" She asked.

"Neither actually. I'm looking for one of the mechanics, Nate Thompson. Does he still work here?" Deacon asked, breathing a sigh of relief when he realized Bruce was nowhere to be seen.

"Nate? What did you say your name was again?" She asked suspiciously, pulling herself up to her full height, which was significantly shorter than he was. Great, she was trying to be protective of the guy. What the hell? If this was a regular enough occurrence for this small, elderly lady to try and protect him, what kind of a man was Nate? Deacon's heartrate notched up a little higher. He hadn't considered that Nate might not be the best man to be Sonia's parent and role model. Was that the real reason Layla had tried to force Sonia on him? The idea of Layla trying to

140

be a protective mother was at odds with what he knew of her selfish lifestyle and personality. Layla only looked out for Layla. He took a deep breath and answered her probing question.

"I didn't," he smiled and shoved his hands in his pockets, hoping to seem less threatening. "I'm-."

"Deacon Kitsman," a loud voice boomed, and Deacon winced. Instantly on high alert as he turned to face the man that had stepped inside the glass door behind him.

"I changed my name years ago. I prefer Deacon Mackenzie," he responded and watched the conflicted emotions wash over his former stepfather's face.

Bruce was shorter than he remembered and hadn't aged well. His once charming smile now only seemed oily and forced. Deacon was a full head taller than him now, and it was odd to be staring down at the man that had terrorized his mother for years. He wanted to punch the man in his face, but instead kept them firmly in his pocket and forced himself to stay calm.

"Right. Sorry, I forgot. Hard habit to get into, thinking of you as someone other than my son," Bruce replied blinking and crossing the room to offer a hand. Deacon reluctantly shook it. "What brings you down here? Looking for a new ride?"

"He came by to talk to Nate," the woman behind the desk answered.

"Nate? What for?" Bruce asked, surprised. "I had no idea you guys knew each other."

"It's a private matter. I'd rather not discuss it with anyone else," Deacon's eye started twitching. Was anyone going to answer him? "Is he here or not?"

141

"Yeah, he's here. Look, Deacon, before you go, please listen to me for a minute," Deacon let Bruce pull him aside, not really wanting to listen to whatever he had to say. But he would if it was the only way to get to Nate. That little girl was all that mattered to him right at this moment, so he pushed his loathing and irritation and disgust down, unwilling to open that box and exam those pieces of himself, and buried it while he listened to what Bruce had to say. "I'm sorry for what I put you and your mom through. It couldn't have been easy living with me back then. I've gotten help for my issues, and I've been sober and clean since the day you left. It was a real wake-up call that the boy I'd raised as my son wanted nothing to do with me once you found out I wasn't your real dad. I was replaced by your real father and a new stepfather who is a million times better for both of you. I could never compete with them, but I should have treated you and your mom better that I did, and I'm sorry. If you can ever find it in your heart to forgive me, I'd love to take you out for some coffee maybe and talk more sometime," the older man smiled, his eyes filled with hope. Deacon didn't have the heart say no and walk away. After all, it hadn't all been bad, and he did have some fond memories of playing catch with him and even camping in the backyard. Deacon found himself smiling back and nodding as he remembered some of his happier childhood memories.

"I think I can do that," he answered. "But right now, I really need to talk to Nate."

"Sure, sure. Of course. He's in the break room at the back. Do you remember where to go?" Bruce asked, glancing distractedly at the couple that had entered the small office.

"Yeah, I'll see myself back there," Deacon watched for a moment as Bruce jogged the short distance to his potentially new clients.

He glanced over at the empty desk where the woman had stood a few moments earlier. Since she'd disappeared, he turned his attention to the short hallway before him and headed in the direction of the breakroom. It was strange being back here after all these years. Nothing had changed, except he was older and bigger now, so the offices were suddenly smaller and incredibly confining. The sooner he was out of here and back on his spacious farm, the better he would feel.

The break room was empty except for a single man, sitting with his feet propped up on the ancient table, a grease covered baseball cap over his face as he rocked back on his chair. Deacon quickly appraised him, noticing his build and colouring were like Sonia's. He took a deep breath and purposely pulled a chair out as noisily as possible, the legs scratching the floor with an ear-splitting shriek that had Nate losing his balance and sent him crashing to the linoleum floor.

"What the FUCK?" Nate shouted, barely avoiding smacking his head off the water cooler next to him.

"Sorry about that. Didn't meant to startle you," Deacon replied calmly, taking a seat as Nate picked himself up and fixed his chair. He waited patiently as the man settled himself at the table again before speaking. "Are you Nate Thompson?"

"Yeah, what about it? I don't need to ask who you are," Nate spat, crossing his arms over his chest. "Nice to know that you know who I am, finally."

"You here to chew me out about Layla?" Nate barked the question, his leg bouncing as he sat staring at the wall in front of

143

him. Deacon sized him up for a moment, letting him stew in his guilt and suspicions before replying. The man was taller than he was, and muscular, but Deacon suspected he'd have the upper hand in a fight with Nate, even without his military background, if this conversation turned to blows. Deacon fought his way through middle school, when the other kids tormented him with photos of his mom and Alex caught having sex by the paparazzi after they met in Mexico. He'd learned fast how to throw a punch that usually ended a fight before it began. The years of hard work on the farm had made his body stronger, and helped keep his mind clear through high school, and performing in dives full of drunk people for years had only honed his skills. Had to be fast if the rowdy crowd turned violent, or he would have been eaten alive years ago. Nate's height and longer reach were the only thing he had going for him as far as Deacon could tell.

"Nope. Layla cheated on me, that's on her. You, however, have a big problem and I'm here to see how serious you are about fixing that," Deacon finally responded. "I know Sonia's not my daughter, even if Layla keeps insisting that she is. I now also believe the threats she's held over my head for all these years was a bald-faced attempt to hold onto something that wasn't hers to hold on to. I didn't know who Sonia's real father was until the other day. In fact, for the last ten years I half-believed, half-feared her lies were truth and my stepfather was Sonia's sperm donor."

"Is that why you never denounced her? I always wondered about that. I've been trying to claim my daughter for years, but I can't afford the fancy lawyers to fight her and with your name on Sonia's birth certificate, I don't have a legal leg to stand on," Nate replied. "I figured there was a possibility that Sonia was actually yours, but my heart refused to believe it. How do you know she isn't your daughter?"

144

"I was away on tour opening for another band. We'd been gone for a few months when Layla broke the news. Timing didn't match up nearly close enough to be half-way convincing." Deacon explained.

"I don't get it. Why would she do this?" Nate asked, rubbing his chin. "It doesn't make any sense."

"Layla latched on to me in high school. I thought it was because of my guitar skills, or that I was in this super cool band with my best friends. We worked hard all through senior year to land gig after gig after graduation, and when we were discovered by a record label, it was the icing on the cake. Then I found out she was only using me to get closer to my stepdad, Superstar, A-list, British Actor Xander Hawkins." Deacon relayed the entire tale of what had happened between him and Layla, fighting the bitterness that burned the back of his throat as he talked, and surprisingly enough Nate sat there listening and nodding, only asking the occasional question.

"A DNA test could have solved this problem years ago," Nate replied sourly. "But I don't see how any of this is going to help me get custody of my baby girl. I don't earn enough money working here to hire a lawyer, but I can't leave town to find a better paying job either. Layla might take Sonia and leave at any moment if she thought no one was watching her. Especially now that her mom's dying of cancer and can't keep raising Sonia anymore."

"I'd like to help you with the legal fees if that's alright with you. I think Sonia needs her real dad in her life, and you clearly care a lot about her, or you would have walked away years ago. I know better men who have," Deacon leaned forward as he said this, watching the emotions war across Nate's face as he heard it. "My parents were dumb kids when they had me, and my bio-dad abandoned us before he even knew about me. They made a lot of mistakes, but one thing I know, is that leaving is the biggest regret he's had to live with. It took a lot of guts for him to come back when he did and face the mistakes he made. It took a lot of guts for you to stick around and try to be a dad to a child whose mother has done everything she can to push you away. I can't keep letting her control all of our lives and hurting everyone in the process."

"I can't possibly let you do that," Nate replied, standing so quickly his chair crashed to the floor behind him. "I'll figure something out. I refuse to take hand-outs."

"Even a proud man must set aside his pride for the sake of his child," Bruce spoke quietly from the entryway. Deacon hadn't heard the door open and practically jumped out of his skin. He squeezed his eyes shut as he fought for control of his nerves, repeating to himself that he was safe. He was home, and he was safe. No one was trying to kill him here. His heart rate slowly returned to normal as he soothed his nerves enough to listen. No one noticed his inner turmoil and he sighed with relief as Bruce continued to talk.

"It's a lesson I learned the hard way. Why didn't you mention any of this before? I could have found extra shifts for you or worked something out to help you get that lawyer," Bruce offered.

"Like I said, I don't accept hand-outs," Nate repeated, irritably. "And I don't air out my dirty laundry in public. It's my problem, my child. I'll take care of it somehow."

"It's not a hand-out if you help me out during the harvest. I inherited Mackenzie Orchards recently, and could use the help," Deacon offered. "But if you don't want it, I'm sure Sonia will

146

love living on a farm. After all that Layla's done, she's clearly proven she's unfit to raise her daughter, and since she keeps claiming I'm the girl's father, I guess that leaves it up to me to fix that situation. It's in Sonia's best interest after all."

Deacon rose from his chair with a shrug and started for the door. He nodded at Bruce on his way out the door and grinned when heard Nate shout at him to wait.

Chapter 24

*"It hurts like hell to lose the one you love. The one piece of
your soul that you feel incomplete without. But planting my new
orchard... the hard work that's nearly back breaking... the
sweat... there's something to be said about work helping to ease
your mind. I fall asleep every night, too exhausted to dream. But I
find myself thinking of Rose less and less these days. I'm looking
for my second chance. I hope it's out there waiting for me."* -
Travis's journal

Amaira stretched and climbed out of bed. Changing into her
workout clothes, she lazily strolled into her living room and made
herself a protein shake before pulling out her yoga mat and laying
it out on her balcony. Sighing, she took a sip then stretched out
on the mat and worked through her morning routine. It was still
early enough that the fresh air still had a slight chill and she
relished it, closing her eyes, and imagining herself back on the
farm. Her mind was clear of the fog it had been in for days, and
she was finally at peace… until the honking of car horns and
screeching of tires reminded her that she wasn't in the orchard
anymore. Her inner peace disrupted, she packed up and headed
inside to shower and start her day. Her boss was expecting a
script, and she didn't have anymore time to waste. Being a
screenwriter was her dream, it was what she'd worked her entire
adult life to accomplish. Now that the opportunity had finally
arose to see some of her work come to life on the silver screen,
she refused to let it pass her by. There were thousands of writers

out there hoping their scripts would be chosen, and their movies would be made. This was the chance of a lifetime.

Hopping out of the shower, she quickly dressed and finished unpacking her bag. Her fingers brushed against something cool and hard. Frowning, she pulled it out and gasped. Deacon's grandfather's journal had somehow gotten mixed up in her belongings when she'd packed. She would have to find a way to return it. Perhaps she could give it back to Alex the next time she saw him in the office. Setting it aside, she finished up what she was doing and stepped into the living room. Cracking her laptop, she settled in at her desk with a giant mug of French Pressed Coffee with hazelnut cream, a big bag of red licorice and spread out her notes. Her college boyfriend had often joked about how she was the perfect mix of adult and child whenever she was on a deadline for her English classes. He wasn't wrong. She twirled a piece of licorice around her finger and took a bite, contemplating where to start.

"How am I going to piece all of this together?" She asked herself, her fingers tapping on the desk as she tried to visualize the story she wanted to tell. She started to type out a rough outline, the clicking of the keys like music to her ears, then paused to review what she'd written.

"This is total trash," she growled to her empty apartment and deleted the entire paragraph. The morning continued in this fashion, the sunlight growing brighter as the day wore on, with Amaira writing and deleting everything she started. Nothing seemed right, and all she could think of was the journal in her bedroom, beckoning her to read it. Giving up, she closed her laptop and skulked into the next room to retrieve it, then made a fresh pot of coffee and settled in on her cozy egg swing on the apartment balcony overlooking the street below. The journals brittle pages crinkled as she gently flipped through them searching for the last page she'd read. The wispy scent of stale cologne wrapped around her like a familiar warm blanket as the Mackenzie's late patriarch's journal transported her back in time and back to the farm that she never thought she would miss so much.

I hate feeling so useless all the time. Especially when Sarah cries for her mommy. Now the Henderson's are even talking of selling their farm and retiring to Florida. That means my land is going to end up next to some huge suburban development and the town's going to grow and grow until it's bursting at the seams. That might be good for businesses around here, but what about the other farmers, like me, who would only end up squeezed out of their land by the vast urban sprawl. People will be all over my land, treating it like public property and destroying my crops. I can't let that happen, but I don't know how to stop it. All this change is gnawing on my mind. What am I going to do?

Amaira sighed, hoping things would get better as she flipped the page, but also relishing in the sadness and twisting emotions that mirrored her own.

Trent's really done it this time. Just as we put in that joint offer on the Henderson farm, he announces that him and his new bride are jumping ship and moving to the states so his wife can be closer to her family. To make matters worse, he's decided to enlist in the fucking army! Who does that? He says he needs a stable income now, and more space for his family. His growing family, apparently. Why can't he do that here? I don't understand any of this. We just put in that offer on the Henderson farm! Why can't they live there? It's practically right next door. Family should stay together. Sarah could use a cousin to grow up with. All she's got is that Jeffries boy, Jackson. He's a good kid, and despite his mother's bitterness over loosing my brother years ago, Jackson and Sarah are best friends. But it would be good for her to have another girl around.

Smiling, Amaira flipped the page. Sarah and Jack were still best friends. It was easy to see in their interactions with each other, despite their short-lived romantic past. It was surreal to watch them, knowing they were married to other people, but she understood them. They were all the other had for most of their childhood. It was only natural their relationship would evolve the way it did.

The Henderson's accepted my offer! Despite being outbid by real estate developers that offered them a lot more money, they took my offer! My farm has now practically doubled in size over night. Trent's stayed behind to help me get a plan in place and meet with some farm hands to help with the expansion. I can't thank him enough. I'm sure going to miss my little brother when he leaves to join his family down south. It's one more loss my little girl's going to have to cope with, and that breaks my heart, but this time it's not forever at least. Soon she'll have a cousin, and Trent and his wife have both promised to spend every summer here so they can be together.

Amaira paused her reading to look out over the busy street below and sip her coffee, letting the words wrap around her brain as she envisioned what it must have been like for Travis Mackenzie to first loose his wife, and then his brother, though in much different ways. His life was changing fast, and despite his clear reluctance to let the changes happen, he adapted with them and worked hard to be the best dad he could for his little girl. His love for his daughter saturates the pages of his journal. The beginning of an idea began to form in her mind, and she decided to keep reading, hoping that the idea swirling around inside her would solidify into a half-decent concept for a script.

I'm exhausted from working in the orchard all day and baking with Sarah and my mom in preparation for her school bake sale tonight. I didn't want to go, but my mother talked me into it with her "I'm getting old and frail and need my big strong boy to carry in all these baked goodies," guilt trip. That woman will probably out live us all. Old and frail my ass. I can't believe I bought into her guilt trip, but if I hadn't, I might never have officially met Mary. Turns out she is a teacher at Sarah's school, and she came by our table to buy an apple dumpling.

It's been years since Rose left us, and I haven't given women or relationships much thought. To be completely honest, I never expected the ache over Rose's loss to ever ease enough for me to feel anything for another woman, but Mary has changed all of that. I know I said I was ready for a second chance, but I was bullshitting myself. Until I met Mary, I did nothing but talk about second chances. I never believed one was in the cards for a simple man like me. Yet here it is. Is it too soon to say it's love? Probably, but I can't help how my heart raced every time she came near, or how I seemed to forget how to breathe when she tried to strike up a conversation. She must think I'm nuts or something, because all I did was stare at her until my mother shoved an apple cider donut in my gaping mouth. Then she did the most unbelievable thing. My mother asked Mary out for me! I can't believe she did that. I can still hear her explaining herself to Mary, and all I did was stand there like an idiot and listen as she told her that I was "simply in awe of her beauty and would love to take her to dinner sometime."

I'm a grown man, and I refuse to admit that I needed my mother to ask a woman out on a date for me.... But I'm grateful she did because now I have a date to plan.

Travis's mother seemed like quite the character in her day. Amaira grinned and headed back inside. She needed to get back to work while inspiration was still hot in her veins.

~

"Good morning, Darrell," Amaira smiled tiredly at her boss as she stepped into his small office. It had been months since she'd last been there, and nothing had changed. The great thing about being a writer was that, except for needing to be in the office for meetings, she could work largely from home. Since returning to Los Angeles, she'd spent her time holed up in her apartment writing and polishing the script she clutched in her hands.

"Amaira, welcome back. Is that it then?" Darrell asked, nodding his frog like head towards the package she held in front of her like a shield. Taking a deep breath to calm her nerves, Amaira nodded and placed it in his outstretched hand. It wasn't exactly the story he'd sent her out to the Mackenzie farm to write, but she prayed he liked it. It was her best work, and she'd poured everything she had into writing it.

"Sir, I know I promised a romance inspired by Xander's love match with his wife, and I tried to write it, but I think this is even better. It's still a small-town romance, but it looks at multiple generations of a family that would walk through fire for each other, and the ones they love. It's about second chances, and love at first sight, and the bonds that hold a family together in the wake of tragedy. I really believe you'll like this better than anything I could have written about Xander." She defended her work, anxiety ratcheting through her body as he flipped through the pages. Amaira opened her mouth to say more, the silence in the office nearly deafening, when Darrell held out a hand to stop her.

"I'll look at it tonight and if I like it, I'll send a copy to Xander as well. Don't get your hopes up. Hundreds of scripts pass my desk and into the trash can. But I have to say, I'm disappointed that the first assignment I've given you isn't the idea *you* pitched. I expect more from you in the future. Creativity is what I expect from all my writers, but next time try to use it more in line with what you should be working on. Everything else you do and pitch in your own time. Understand?" Darrell glanced up at her over the rim of his bottle-glasses, his jowls jiggling as he talked.

Amaira nodded.

"I understand. Thank you for reading it," she stepped out of the office, and exhaled the breath she hadn't realized she was holding. All that was left for her to do now was start brainstorming her next pitch. She wasn't sure what she might decide on, the only thing she was certain of, was that she was staying far away from romance. Maybe a horror flick or something? She toyed with the idea as she stepped through the doors of the studio and out into the parking lot, the afternoon heat slamming into her and stealing her breath away after enjoying the airconditioned offices. She climbed into her Jeep Wrangler and cranked the air as she pulled out of her spot and began the journey to her favourite café for a light lunch.

Chapter 25

"Mary... Mary... Mary... God what that woman does to me! I don't deserve her, but I'll spend every day worshipping the woman if she'll let me." -Travis's journal

Deacon groaned, rubbing his aching leg as he climbed out of his truck. The custody battle was brutal, with Layla insisting that he was Sonia's father. It didn't seem to matter to her that DNA proved he wasn't. He considered the idea that Layla had started to believe her own lies. But the tests proved that Nate Thompson was Sonia's biological father. When faced with the hard proof, she still tried to deny it, but it took all the steam out of her accusations and extortion attempts. The judge had sided with him and Nate, and awarded custody of Sonia to her father, too the relief of Sonia's grandmother, as she'd cheered and cried, relieved from the burden of raising her granddaughter and what would happen to Sonia when she died. The judge didn't take kindly to parental alienation and extortion however, and threatened to deny Layla access to her daughter, but Nate had stepped in.

"Your Honour, Layla might not be the best mother, but she's the only one Sonia has. I'd hate to come between them the way that Layla has forced Deacon to come between my daughter and myself. Sonia's going to need her mom, and I'm ok with her having visitation," he'd explained, ignoring the fuming looks Layla sent his way as he spoke.

"Hmph. Fine. She may have supervised visits, with overnight visits to be granted upon completion of the parenting courses I'm mandating her to complete in the next six months. But I will be forwarding the evidence shared here to the proper authorities to investigate her criminal harassment and extortion." The sound of the judge's gavel reverberated through the room with a finality that spoke volumes.

It was over. Everything that Layla had held over his head, all the accusations, the doubt, the hurt and betrayal, it was all over. Deacon breathed a sigh of relief. He clapped Nate on the shoulder to congratulate him and had headed home, filled with a new conviction that he would reclaim his life now that Layla was firmly out of it. The sight of the burly biker on his front porch, with his legs perched on the bannister as he relaxed in the rocking chair and drank a glass of lemonade, had Deacon pulling up short as he rounded the front of his truck.

"Bout time you came home," the gruff voice called out and Deacon grinned, ignoring his aching leg as he bounded up the steps. "Your sister told me I could wait for you out here and brought me this deliciously refreshing drink. I had to decline the four-course meal she offered though. Didn't think I'd be here this long. She's quite the hostess."

"Yeah, just keep your paws off her. She's too young for you," Deacon teased back, easing onto the swing next to him.

"Betty would kill me," Charlie laughed. "Right after she strung me up by the balls and had me drawn and quartered."

"She'd have to get in line behind the protective big brother who'd gut you with a spoon, and feed it to the neighbours' pigs," Deacon chuckled, drawing himself up to his full height and flexing in his most intimidating pose.

"Relax, I'm not into cradle robbing. Betty's more than I can handle as it is, and your sisters were practically mine too after all the time I spent here as a kid." Charlie sipped his lemonade, and

Deacon relaxed back into his seat, barely containing his curiosity over his old friend's sudden visit.

"So… I need to ask. Are you planning on sticking around long?" Charlie asked, staring into his empty glass.

"Yeah. I've been medically discharged from the military. Now that everything's sorted out with Layla and Sonia, I've got no reason to leave. Besides, someone needs to keep this place going. Grandpa didn't leave it to me for it too fall into disrepair or sold for developments. It would kill him if he were still around. Why do you ask?" Deacon watched as a million different emotions crossed his friend's face.

"No reason. It's just… the guys and I have been talking, and we were hoping you might be interested in rejoining the band. It was never the same without you," Charlie answered quietly.

Deacon arched a brow, surprised. He wasn't sure what he'd expected, but it hadn't been this. He pondered the idea of playing in a band again. Rolled it around in his head as he considered the offer.

"What about that other guy? The obnoxious ass I met at the party," he asked, savouring his friend's discomfort as he wormed around in his chair, looking everywhere but at Deacon.

"Dude's a dud, man. All attitude the minute we asked him to play with us. His talent's nothing compared to the magic in your pinkie finger. Besides, he kind of blew a gasket after your birthday party and walked out on us," Charlie shrugged, not meeting Deacon's eye. "Not much of a loss if you ask me, but we're still short a lead singer and guitar player."

Deacon couldn't help the laughter bubbling inside him. He wanted to run inside and share his excitement with Amaira. After all this time, he was finally getting his life back. She was right about refusing to let Layla control him with her lies, and everything was finally going the way they were meant to. Remembering that Amaira was gone filled him with a coldness that turned his lightness into a giant stone that lodged in his throat, choking him as he tried to get the words out. Instead, he rose from his chair, clapped his buddy on the shoulder and collected his glass. He stepped inside the house, needing a minute to collect himself before returning with a new glass of lemonade for Charlie, and one for himself. Almost everything was working out in his favour. He would gladly rejoin his old band, but he still had no idea what to do about Amaira. It had been weeks since she'd left, and she still refused to answer his calls and texts. His sisters were pissed at him still over Amaira leaving, but he was positive they'd get over it eventually. The question was, would Amaira ever forgive him?

⌒﹏

Deacon took a deep breath, calming his nerves before pressing the buzzer. The wrought iron gate swung open, and he drove through it and pulled up in front of the massive stone manor with its four-car garage and a pool house that he couldn't see but knew was there. Shortly after they'd gotten married, his mother and Alex had gutted the house that had been here when they bought it, and the old brewery on the other side of the property that now made his mom's hard cider, and completely remodeled it to be their dream home. Next to the house in Malibu, it was the only home his siblings remembered. He smiled, staring up at the house and remembering what his grandpa had said the first time he'd seen it after it was completed.

"Damn thing isn't large enough for your ego, Alex. But given everything you've put my baby girl through, it'll do," and with

159

that he'd clapped Alex on the shoulder and asked Deacon to give him and Grandma Mary a tour.

He could almost hear Alex and Grandpa Travis arguing as he walked through the door. It was strange being back here after so many years away, yet nothing had changed beyond the wall colours. He strode through the empty corridor, his footsteps echoing as he wandered through the house, searching for his family. He found Riley alone in the cozy family room in the basement, playing video games online and shouting into a headset. Riley paused the game as Deacon entered the room.

"Hey, where is everyone?" Deacon asked.

"Mom's busy with some cider trouble or something. She's been locked in her office all day, but she'll be out soon. She never misses family dinners. Dad's out back on the barbecue, Amy's out shopping with friends, I think but she's due back anytime now. What's up?" Riley stretched out in his chair his headset now forgotten on the table.

"Just came to get a few things. Mind if I hang out a bit?" Deacon sank down into the sofa when Riley shrugged and picked up his headset and controller. The movement drew Deacon's gaze to the table, where he noticed a large stack of papers under Riley's water glass. He'd been around enough movie scripts in his lifetime to recognize one without any trouble, it shouldn't be something new to him, but he still asked his brother about it.

"Dad's next pet project. What do you care? It's not as if you actually cared about the woman who wrote it," Riley accused, unpausing his game. Deacon stared at it, curiosity burning a whole in his brain until he succumbed to temptation and reached for it, moving Riley's glass to the table as he did so. Amaira had written it. This was the script she wrote about his family. He sat back, and casually flipped it open to peruse it while his brother pointedly ignored him.

Her writing grabbed his attention almost immediately, and he found himself transported back in time to when his grandfather met his second wife. She'd used his grandfather's journal for inspiration, as he'd hoped she would, but he hadn't expected this. He flipped the page, drinking in her words and his grandfather's memories. Soon the story morphed into his mother's story, how she'd fallen in love with his dad, and married the wrong man out of spite, how she'd divorced him and fallen in love with Xander Hawkins. The entire story soon blended into his story, with his music career falling apart because of one woman's infidelities and toxic personality and causing him to push away the woman who'd seen through all his scars and loved him anyway. It was a story about second chances. Was that what she wanted? Had she hoped he would see this and come find her? He didn't dare hope that it was some coded message to him, but the story was a message showing that no matter the circumstances, second chances at love were real and did happen.

Deacon stared blankly at the last page, unaware of his mother calling them out to dinner on the patio. His family was right, he was a complete fool for pushing Amaira away. He had to make it right, but how when she wouldn't answer his calls? He could go to Los Angeles and talk to her in person, but he had no clue where she lived. The only clue he had was that she lived in an apartment above a fancy coffee shop, but that didn't really help him. There had to be hundreds of buildings like that in LA. Then it dawned on him. He didn't have to find her apartment at all. Not when he knew where she worked. He hated the idea of ambushing her at work, but he needed to talk to her somehow and it was the only idea he had, short of hiring a private investigator or a skywriter to share his apology with the world.

Engrossed in making plans for his trip to LA, Deacon forgot about dinner and flew out of the den and up the stairs to his old bedroom. He flipped open the laptop on the desk, googled the studio's address, and booked himself a plane ticket. He heard his mom calling him down again for dinner and grinned. He was a grown man and his mother still treated him like his siblings sometimes, always making sure he ate enough or was taking care of himself. He hadn't realized how much he'd missed it until that moment. Grabbing his guitar case and a couple items from his old room, he carried them downstairs and left them by the front door before joining his family. At some point he'd missed his sister returning from the mall and raised his eyebrows at the number of bags she'd abandoned on the kitchen table.

"Hey, what smells delicious out here?" He asked as he stepped through the glass doors that led off the kitchen, and out onto the stone patio surrounding the inground pool.

"We've got steak for the adults, and burgers for the kids. Pick your poison," Alex replied, flipping a burger on the grill, the grease making the flames sizzle and pop.

"How did court go?" His mom asked, handing him a bottle of hard cider.

"It went better than I expected," the bottle made a popping sound as he opened it and took a sip. "Wow, have you changed the recipe?

"I tweaked it a little," his mom grinned and filled her plate with a steak and salad. "What do you think?"

"It's fantastic," he replied taking another sip. "Nate, Sonia's real dad, now has full custody and Layla needs to complete several parenting courses if she ever wants overnight or unsupervised visitation with their daughter. She might also be

162

facing criminal charges if the judge has his way. He's opened a criminal investigation into her conduct, so don't be surprised if an investigator comes around asking questions."

"That's no less than she deserves after the stunt she pulled," Alex commented, turning off the grill and joining them. "Your mum explained how Layla manipulated you into paying her child support all these years. I'm sorry you had to go through all that, but I'm even more sorry if I've ever given you cause to believe I would mistreat my family like that."

"No, it wasn't anything you did. There's nothing to be sorry about," Deacon shook his head. "It's my own baggage that she used to manipulate me. You've never given me cause to think you would cheat on my mother. I'm sorry that I didn't realize that sooner and let her poison me against you."

"Don't worry about it. I've got pretty thick skin," Alex clapped Deacon on the shoulder, and gave it a reassuring squeeze. "Although now that I think of it, there is something you can do to make it up to me."

"Sure, what is it?" Deacon asked, loading his plate with salad, corn on the cob, and a nice juicy steak. He pulled out a chair at the table and sat down across from his mom. Alex turned off the barbecue and after loading his own plate and insisting that Amy and Riley stop horsing around and eat before their food grew cold, he joined them.

"So, I've received Amaira's script, and I've been trying to picture who I think should be casted for it. The problem is that it's a hugely intimate story based on our family," Alex paused and took a bite of his steak.

"Yeah, I kind of snuck a look at it. Hope you don't mind. It was sitting on the coffee table, and I couldn't resist reading it. It's good, I hope you don't decide to hide it away in a vault or something," Deacon replied. "Have you read it mom?"

"I have," Sarah answered. "I quite enjoyed it and it made me feel connected to your grandparents again. Almost like they never left."

"So, what does any of this have to do with me?" Deacon asked, turning his attention back to his stepfather.

"There's this scene where the couple is dancing, and I was hoping maybe you could get your old band to perform in it? Of course, you'd have to audition for it, to avoid any accusations of favouritism, but I really can't think of anyone else who'd fit that scene so well."

"You're sure you want me? I haven't played seriously with a band in years, and we haven't had a practice yet. Charlie *just* asked me to come back. I don't even know if the rest of the band is able to go on the road again. Some of them might have families now, but… I guess I can ask them tomorrow night at practice. Can we stay at the Malibu house during auditions? It might help to convince them to go if they don't have extra expenses and lavish quarters to stay in."

"I'll give you the keys before you leave tonight. You know, you've never had to ask to stay there. It's your home just as much as this one is," Alex responded.

"Thanks, Alex. I appreciate that. I admit, I've never felt comfortable there, I'm too much of a country boy I guess," Deacon and Alex grinned at each other and allowed silence to descend around them as they turned their attention to the food on their plates.

Deacon couldn't remember the last time he'd enjoyed a home cooked meal with his family. Something else he hadn't realized he'd missed and spent the evening chatting and wandering around the house reliving old memories. It was dark by the time he bid good night to everyone and headed back to his farm. *His farm.* He still felt weird calling it that. In his mind it would always be his grandfather's farm. The home of the strongest man he'd ever known, the man whose voice had spurred Deacon to action out on the battlefield and saved his life.

He pulled in the driveway and shut the truck off. The house was dark, and he sat there staring at it for a few minutes, wishing he was back with his family or coming home to Amaira's waiting embrace. His war wounds didn't hurt as much as realizing he might not be able to fix the damage, he'd caused to their relationship. If there even was a relationship anymore. She'd left pretty fast after that fight on his birthday. Pushing aside the hurt that knifed through his gut, Deacon climbed out of his truck, grabbed his guitar case, and headed to the barn instead.

Chapter 26

"Jimmy's a pretty hard worker. One of my best farm hands. I wonder if he'd be ok with me making him foreman. I'm going to need someone to take over while I'm gone. That is, if everything goes off without a hitch and Mary says yes at dinner like I hope she will. She's mentioned always wanting to go to British Columbia and travel down the west coast all the way to California. I think that sounds like the perfect honeymoon." - Travis's journal

"I can't believe we're in Malibu! Barely a couple days back with the band and already you're bringing in bigger gigs than we've seen since you left," Betty gushed, her eyes bulging as she took in their surroundings. Deacon grinned as he followed the rest of the guys inside his family's West Coast home, grateful for the opportunity for his band to stay here during auditions and possibly longer.

"Nothing's set in stone. Remember, Alex said we needed to audition first," he reminded her.

"Sure, sure. And our being here has nothing to do with you being a giant jerk that's trying to fix things with Amaira. You really screwed up. Have you thought about how you're going to win her back?" Betty asked.

"Betty, stay out of it," Charlie loudly whispered, setting their bags down in the entryway and following her into the next room.

"Stay out of what? He already knows he doesn't deserve her and he's a giant jerk-hole. I'm not telling him anything new,"

Betty placed her hands on her hips and tapped her toe, staring at Charlie over the edge of her Audrey Hepburn sunglasses.

"Babe," Charlie crossed the room and wrapped his arms around her. "It doesn't matter what he knows, what matters is that he's here to man up to his mistakes. Give him a break."

Betty sighed, practically melting into Charlie's embrace.

"Betty's right," Deacon announced, breaking up the intimate moment. "I am an idiot for pushing her away, and I have no idea how to fix it. Other than trying to talk to her while we're here so I can at least apologize for how I acted."

"I don't think you should apologize," Betty announced, stepping away from her husband. "At least, not right away. When we get this part, we could be here for a couple weeks while the production company sorts things out and starts filming."

"So, what do you suggest?" Deacon asked, collapsing on the sofa.

"You need to woo her. Win her back and *then* apologize for being the world's biggest ass," she replied bluntly.

"Babe-." Charlie started, but Betty cut him off with a glare.

"I'm not telling him anything he doesn't know," she repeated caustically, and turned back to Deacon. "First, get this part in her film. The rest, we'll figure out as we go. I'm going to find my room."

Charlie and Deacon watched as she turned and stormed out of the room. It was strange for Deacon to be back in this house, after a decade of living in bunkers and tents, swearing that he'd never step foot in anything owned by Xander Hawkins ever again. Funny how time and space can change one's perspective. Ten years ago, he'd believed the worst and hated his stepfather. Now he had nothing but love for the man that stepped up for him and his mom and accepted him as one of his own children.

"Sooooo…" Charlie broke the silence that had descended around them with Betty's departure. "I know Betty was a bit harsh but she's not wrong. A woman like Amaira isn't going to accept a simple apology, so what's the plan?"

"I have no idea. I was hoping once we got here, I'd know exactly what to do and say, but I'm just as confused now as I was before," Deacon sank onto an extravagant wingback chair and hid his face in his palms.

"When I was dating Betty, I screwed up really bad. I was drunk, maybe more than a little high, and some groupie started giving me a lap dance. Betty caught us and nearly tore off my balls before storming out on me. When I finally sobered up, I thought that was the end of us and it nearly destroyed me. I realized I couldn't live without her, so I started writing her little love notes and I'd leave them everywhere that was special to us with instructions on how and when to find the next note. When she found the last note, I knew we were going to be ok. She never would have pursued all those letters if there wasn't some love for me still in her heart. I made a giant circle with tonnes of candles on the beach where we'd gone for our first date, and I stood in the middle with my heart in my hands and told her exactly how I felt and how sorry I was."

"Wow, who knew you were such a romantic!" Deacon teased. "Amaira and I don't have any special places in LA for me to leave her love notes. I don't think that would work for us."

"Maybe not, but if we get this role on her film, maybe you could use that to your advantage. Writers have to be onsite for last minute script changes, don't they?"

An idea started to form in Deacon's mind, and he jumped off the couch, searching for a pen and paper to write it down on before he forgot it. Wordlessly, he handed it to Charlie and paced the room anxiously while his friend read and re-read it.

"It's not our typical style, but I like it. Let's grab the guitars and work out the melody," Charlie rose from his seat and Deacon followed him out of the room, a smile forming on his lips.

"You think it'll work?" He asked as they grabbed their guitar cases from the entryway and Deacon led him to the soundproof room Alex had built for him when he'd started learning to play. He could play here as often as he wanted, day or night, and not worry about waking his brother and sister when they were still little. Next to accepting him as part of the family and being a dad to him when he didn't have to, it was the best gift Alex could have given him. Now that he thought about it, he couldn't believe how easy it was for someone like Layla to manipulate him so easily and nearly destroy their relationship. He vowed to make it up to his stepdad somehow, right after he apologized to Amaira the only way he knew how.

"Alright everyone. This is it. Thank you for coming to the audition. Musicians are to the right, actors to the left. Sorry ladies, we've already found our leading lady for this one, but feel free to audition for one of the smaller parts," a bald man in his forties announced to the crowd gathered in the waiting room. He indicated the doors on either side of him. "Hand over your portfolios and resumes, and the completed applications to my assistant here and we'll see each of you in the order that she calls your name."

Betty squealed with excitement.

"I can't believe this is really happening! You guys are going to kill these auditions," she kissed Charlie and practically danced on the spot.

Deacon couldn't quell the nerves that threatened to eat him from the inside out. There were a lot of people here. He hadn't realized auditions would be quite like this, but he was glad Alex hadn't simply given his band the part. They'd always worked hard for the successes they'd had, playing in every dive with a stage they could find until they'd been scouted by a talent scout looking for bands to open for music festivals across the East Coast. They were once on their way, might even be big names by now if he hadn't let his personal demons get in the way. Suddenly, he realized he wanted this not just for him and Alex, but for his friends, his band, for Betty and Charlie, the best of friends. He owed it to them.

The casting director's assistant collected their applications and directed them to the right with out a glance up at them, while another collected the pile and took them into the room where the casting directors waited. Hours passed before their names were called. Betty squealed again and gave each of them a hug for encouragement.

"You got this in the bag, guys," she gushed as they entered the room.

Deacon took his place in front of the microphone and strapped on his guitar. He quickly checked the tune, despite having checked it a hundred times while they waited. Nervously, he cleared his throat and waited for the casting director's attention before introducing himself and the band and began to play. He shut his eyes, allowing himself to get lost in the melody and lyrics, opening them when the song came to an end, and someone cleared their throat. A couple of the casting director's assistants were dabbing their eyes with a tissue, but the bald man sitting directly in front of them simply stared at him with pursed lips. He broke eye contact to write something down and pass it amongst the others at the table. The silence stretched on, and Deacon shifted from one foot to the other, unsure what to say or do next. He cleared his throat, tossing a nervous glance at the rest of the band. Nervously, he cleared his throat again and stepped back up to the microphone to thank them for their time, when the bald man stood and walked over to them, clapping slowly. He came to a stop in front of Deacon and held his hand out for Deacon to shake.

"On behalf of Film Hawk Productions, I'd like to formally offer you and your band a role on our next feature film," he announced with a smile.

Deacon grinned back and shook his hand enthusiastically, opening his mouth to thank him, but the man cut him off before he could get a word out.

"I'd also like to offer you the lead male role if you think you're up for it," he said, cutting off Deacon's reply before he could speak. "Ever do any acting?"

"No," Deacon drew out the word, shock radiating through his body as he replayed the man's offer in his head. "But I grew up around one. How hard could it be?"

"You'd be surprised. Welcome to Hollywood gentlemen," he announced and clapped once before turning and exiting the room,

171

his entourage following closely behind him. Within minutes, Deacon was completely alone with his friends in the giant room that resembled his high school gymnasium.

"Did you hear that, boys?" Charlie hollered, drawing everyone's attention to him as he grabbed Betty and pulled her tightly to his side. "Welcome to Hollywood!"

Chapter 27

"I'm going crazy in anticipation of our date tonight. I'm going to pop the question. THE BIG QUESTION. The question I never in a million years thought I'd be asking again. I hope Rose doesn't resent me for moving on, wherever she is." -Travis's journal

She was going crazy. That had to be it. It was the only explanation for why she keeps seeing Deacon's broad shoulders or smile everywhere she turned lately. It's been months since they'd parted. Why now? She wondered what he was doing and if he was thinking of her too. Shaking her head, she realized he was probably married to that bitch Layla or something stupid like that by now. It's been months, she shouldn't still care, let alone be thinking of him constantly. It had to be the atmosphere on set. She hadn't anticipated the effect filming on a farm would have on her. Especially one designed to be a close cousin to Mackenzie Orchards. That must be it, she decided. The setting is dredging up old feelings and memories. There was absolutely no reason for Deacon to be here. Maybe she should have taken her sister-in-law's suggestion and gone on that blind date after all.

She turned her attention back to the cast list in front of her and frowned. Under male lead, it read D.M., and she wracked her brain trying to remember an actor going by initials only, but nothing that came up with those same letters. Darrel had mentioned he was new to Hollywood and promptly insisted she re-write the party scene to have the male lead also be part of the band that would be performing. It was all too close to the last time she'd laid eyes on Deacon, and her chest squeezed with the memory. He'd also scrapped the title, *Born of Fire,* in favour of

173

his own title *Trials of the Heart.* Apparently, her title sounded too much like an action movie instead of the romance that it was. It sucked, but she went with it. He was the boss after all.

"Alright folks let's get some B-roll and call it a wrap for the night," the director called out. Amaira rose from her chair, clutching her copy of the script and a pencil case, and stretched. It was day two of filming and she still hadn't even caught a glimpse of the actor they'd hired to play Trevor the grief-stricken widower and single dad, but all the backstage gossip agreed that his smile was simply panty melting and he seemed to be completely unaware of the effect he had on all the ladies here and a few of the men. She ignored the voice in her head questioning why she wasn't the least bit curious and headed back to the trailer that was set up as office space for her to work in along with her co-writer Maria who'd been assigned all the scenes with the new actor. If she was a suspicious person, she might think someone was trying to keep her away from him. She chuckled at the idea, ridiculing herself as she opened the trailer door and climbed inside. Maria squealed as she came around her side of the large desk and started gesturing wildly and talking a mile a minute.

"Wait, slow down Maria. I can't keep up. What's all the excitement about?" She asked when Maria paused to take a breath. Maria pointed to the flowers on her desk.

"Those arrived for you an hour ago. They're from a Secret Admirer," she squealed. "He wants you to meet him tomorrow night in the orchard after they finish filming the frost scene. Isn't that romantic?"

"A secret admirer?" Amaira repeated, stunned. She wanted to be as excited as Maria, but she couldn't find the energy. She read over the card that she'd snatched from Maria's waving hand and read it over and over.

174

"So, are you going to go?" Maria asked.

"Go where?"

"To the orchard, silly!"

"Nah, it's probably a joke or actor trying to get me to write him more lines or something," Amaira replied, plopping down in her chair, and staring at the bouquet of sunflowers and brightly coloured chrysanthemums.

"Are you kidding?! You aren't the least bit interested in what he has to say or who he is?" Maria asked, her mouth gaping in shock. "Are you ok? I mean, if you're coming down with something I'd gladly spread the word so whoever he is, doesn't think he's been stood up. Come on Amaira, you have to go!"

"What if he's a slug or troll or something?" Amaira replied listlessly. "I'm not up for being manipulated or romanced. Either way, there's no point in going."

"Look," Maria propped herself up on the edge of her desk, staring at Amaira over her horn-rimmed glasses. "When you get to be my age, life will either be a lot of what-ifs or memories. Don't let this be one of those what-if moments. Go! See who he is, find out what he wants. If he's a troll, walk away, no harm done. But if he's not… well… wouldn't that be a what-if that could haunt you the rest of your life? What if he's the one? What if he's the answer to your broken heart?"

"Ok, ok. I'll go!" Amaira snapped. "But you have to be on standby in case he's a creep, ok?"

"It's a deal," Maria smiled. "Now, what are you going to wear?"

Amaira groaned and dropped her head into her arms on the desk in front of her. What was she getting herself into?

～⌁～

The stars were high in the sky by the time filming in the orchard wrapped for the night. They'd finished filming the couple's first date in the orchard, a night that lived on in Amaira's memories as the most magical night of her life. The orchard was covered in ice, with giant fans blowing to keep it cold enough to bring the scene to life. Ice covered real and fake fruit and leaves, the trees resembling frozen fountains as she picked her way over cables and around lights and various filming equipment. Shouts from the crew as they packed up grew quieter the deeper, she ventured into the orchard.

"This isn't right," she whispered, her voice hoarse from unshed tears. "I shouldn't be here. I'm not ready for this."

"Damn, whoever he was did a real number on you," Maria muttered from beside her. "Look, I'm not out here in the middle of the night freezing my ass off for you for nothing. You're doing this."

Maria grabbed her arm and tugged her along. Amaira reluctantly followed behind her, until a golden flicker nearby brought them both to a stop. Maria squealed excitedly, reminding Amaira of a chihuahua crossing its little legs and yapping to go outside because it must pee every five minutes.

"Oh, come on, you're not even a little bit excited?" Maria paused and arched a brow when she noticed Amaira side-eyeing her. Amaira sighed and pinched her fingers together.

"Maybe a little bit," she replied and ran a hand through her hair to free it from knots. "How's my makeup? Do I look alright?"

"Honey, you look gorgeous. Now go get him," she pushed Amaira forward and stepped into the trees, using the darkness to conceal herself the way they'd agreed in case she needed rescuing.

Amaira took a deep breath, trying to calm the riot of butterflies in her stomach as she stepped forward into the clearing. Her eyes took a moment to adjust as she took in the flickering candles and flowers arranged artfully in a circle around a man she instantly recognized. Fearing her mind was playing tricks on her, she blinked several times, but the man never wavered or changed. He stood before her, still in his costume of denim and plaid, a guitar strung over his shoulders as he started to play. Amaira was frozen to the spot, unable to make sense of anything that was happening before her. He couldn't possibly be here, on her movie set, in costume, serenading her... could he? Suddenly everything started to make sense. All the little glimpses she'd caught of him on set when she thought she was losing her mind, the initials D.M. on the scripts... she wasn't crazy after all.

"Deacon," she breathed his name, her voice barely above a whisper. He ignored her and continued to play and sing as he circled her. From somewhere beyond the trees, a band joined in with him, startling her. She turned and squinted into the trees but couldn't see through the veil of darkness that surrounded them. The sound of his voice brought her back to the moment and she turned to face him again, her heart pounding in her chest harder with every drumbeat.

I'm strumming these strings of this beat up guitar.

Dreaming of Deacon

My fingers are raw.

Like the strings of my heart,

As I lay myself bare to you.

Dance with me in the moonlight.

Dance like we did that night.

When everything seemed so right.

Dance with me in our crystal palace.

This palace made of ice.

Dance with me in the moonlight.

As I lay my heart bare to love's plight.

Come dance with me.

Dance with me.

In the moonlight.

Dance with me.

Dance with me.

Help me melt this palace of ice.

Amaira, you changed my life.

Dreaming of Deacon

You changed my life.

And you opened my heart to love again.

You changed my life.

Let us melt this ice.

Come dance with me.

The song ended, the sounds of his guitar strings dying off in the distance as his fingers stilled. Deacon silently unstrapped his guitar and carefully set it against a tree before facing her. Amaira was speechless, uncertain of what to say or do. This was the most romantic thing anyone had ever done for her.

"Amaira, I've never been great with apologies, but I know I owe you about a million of them. The biggest thing I'm sorry about, is that I pushed you away. You didn't deserve that, or the hurtful things I said. There are so many things I could say, so many reasons to explain why I did and said those things, but the fact is I never should have said them. You were right, and deep down I knew it, but I wasn't ready to face it, and I'm sorry. I was a coward and I'm sorry I couldn't be the man you needed me to be, the man you deserve. I don't deserve a second chance, but I'm going to ask you for one anyway, because I can't live without you. I wake up everyday hoping to see you smiling back at me from the pillow next to mine. I sleep holding your pillow, pretending I can feel the warm of your body lingering on it or the scent of your perfume in the air. Stop me if I start sounding like a stalker," he paused, taking a deep breath and Amaira laughed softly as she stepped closer to him, drawn to him like a moth to a flame, hypnotized by the warm timbre of his voice. "The bottom

179

line, Amaira, is that I love you and I will do anything for just one more dance with you."

"Is that really all you want?" She asked, arching a brow skeptically.

"It's all I dare to ask you for," he answered quietly.

"What about Layla and Sonia?" She asked, needing to know, and at the same time dreading his answer.

"What about them?" he replied. "Sonia is with her real father and Layla is taking court appointed parenting classes. But I don't really want to talk about them right now. I want to talk about us, here and now. So, what do you say? May I have this last dance?"

"Court battles, farming, music and now acting? You've been busy Deacon. Do you really think you have time?" She asked with a small smile on her lips.

"I will always have time to dance with you," he replied and pulled her into his arms. Amaira sighed as she buried her head into his shoulder, music playing around them. For the first time in months, everything in her world was right again.

"Hey Deacon?" She looked up at him as the music ended, not moving out of his arms.

"Did you really do all of this just to apologize and ask me to dance?" She asked.

"You wouldn't answer my calls," he replied with a smile that went straight to her heart. "What else could I do to get your attention?"

"You could have tried talking to me in person," she suggested.

"Nah. You would have walked away, maybe even filed a restraining order if I'd tried that. Besides this is way more romantic," he grinned.

"You might have a point," she giggled. "Now, about that second chance...."

"She said YES!" – Travis's journal

Epilogue

This is it. This was really happening right now. When he auditioned for a small cameo in Trials of the Heart, he never expected this to happen. Now he was sitting with his family, his bandmates, and best friends, waiting anxiously to hear his name be called out. Amaira squeezed his hand reassuringly, and he raised their clasped hands to his lips, kissing their joint fingers. He still couldn't believe she'd given him that second chance, and he woke up every day grateful to be sharing a life with the most incredible woman he'd ever met.

"And the winner of this year's award for best debuting actor goes to…. Deacon Mackenzie!"

There is no other word to describe the reaction of everyone around them but that it was an eruption of chaos. His sisters practically screamed themselves raw, and his brother started chanting his name. It was quickly taken up by everyone at his table, as he rose from his seat, pulling Amaira up with him. He kissed her with all the love in his heart at that moment, to the raucous delight of Charlie and Betty who started hollering at them to break it up and keep it PG for the cameras. Reluctantly, he let her go, grinning at the breathless state she was in as she found her seat again. He turned to the stage and headed down the aisle to accept his award, shaking hands with producers, other actors, and strangers on the way. His co-star, Scarlet Atkins, hugged and congratulated him at the end of the aisle. He quietly thanked her for all her patience with him as he learned how to navigate the world of acting, and before he knew it, he was standing behind the podium, staring out at the hundreds of faces and cameras below him, clutching a golden statue in his hand.

"I honestly don't know what to say," he began. "When I left the army, I never imagined my life would become anything other than that of a simple farmer. Like so many veterans, I was hurt and bitter, determined to spend the rest of my life alone. Life can lead us in the most incredible directions. I barely remember that man anymore, but without him, I never would have gone on this incredible journey to win back the heart of the most unbelievable woman I've ever met. I was determined to win her heart when I auditioned for a small role in the film that she wrote. A film that is inspired by the life of my grandfather, Travis Mackenzie, and my mother and stepfather, Sarah and Xander Hawkins. I can't think of a better tribute to them. This award is really for them, and for my friends who stood by me when I was being a complete tool. I don't know where I'd be without you guys. Thank you. But the true award, for me, is the heart of the woman who wrote Trials of the Heart, Amaira Devan. Amaira, thank you for loving me, for standing by me when I'm being thick headed, and knocking me back down to earth whenever I need the reminder that no matter how famous I get, or how much my head is up in the clouds, I can't fly. I love you, Amaira.

I'd also like to thank Stan Burfew for taking a chance on me and casting me for a role I had no business being cast in. I'm not sure what made you take that chance, but I'm grateful you did. Thank you. Thank you so much everyone. Have a good night!" He bid farewell and waved to the audience as they stood and applauded.

He slung an arm around Amaira's shoulders as he pulled her in close for a kiss on their way out of the building when the ceremony was over. The cool night air washed over his heated flesh, and he sighed with relief, releasing her to help her into one of the waiting limos Xander had rented for the night.

"So, what do want to do now?" Amaira asked, cuddling into him as the limo pulled away from the curb. "There's a few after parties you'll be expected to make an appearance at."

"All I want right now, is to take you home and make love to you for the rest of the night," he replied with a grin.

"You don't want to go out and celebrate?" She asked, surprised.

"I may have won an award tonight, but the real reward is you. I'd do anything for you Amaira. Including renting out the farmhouse to Nate, so he can run the farm with my dad while we stay here to pursue your dreams of writing."

"Really? You would do that for me?"

"I would," he replied soberly. "I love you, Amaira."

"Deacon, I love you, but I don't want to live anywhere else. The farm is a part of you, and I love every part of you. I can write anywhere, but the farm is our home. Besides, you should be closer to your band. You need all the practice you can get if you plan on going on tour again someday" she replied, sliding onto his lap, and pulling his head down until their foreheads touched. "Let's go home."

"Home. I like the sound of that." He whispered, his mouth grazing hers. "I love you so much Amaira."

"I know. I love you too, Deacon. Now shut up and kiss me already," she laughed, pressing her lips and body against his.

"Yes Ma'am." He replied and did exactly that.

THE END

ABOUT THE AUTHOR

Frances Everly has always had an overactive imagination. When she's not writing she's enjoying an eclectic variety of books. She loves writing romance, but she plans to expand into fantasy as F.D. Everly.

Besides a passion for the written word, Frances has an Honors Bachelor of Arts degree in Anthropology. She's also a wife and mother to two wonderful boys.

Follow Frances Everly on TikTok, Facebook, or Instagram

@authorFrancesEverly

Or sign up for the newsletter for exclusive opportunities and keep up with her latest news and projects:

https://mailchi.mp/951c48c5748e/author-frances-everly

Author's Website

HTTP://AuthorFrancesEverly.ca

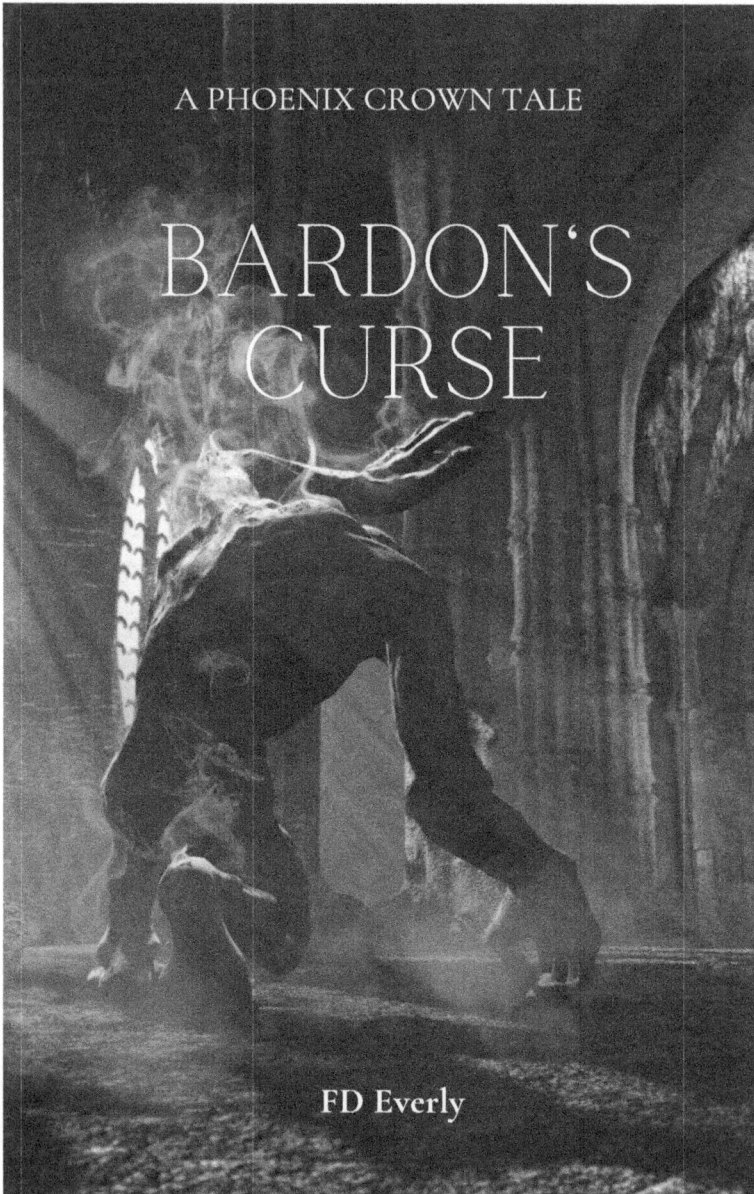

A PHOENIX CROWN TALE

BARDON'S CURSE

FD Everly

Bardon's Curse

By F.D. Everly

There is a curse on the Bardon family. One I wish I'd never learned about. I came upon the knowledge quite by accident one rainy day, while perusing the library for something to read. I found a dusty old, leather-bound book marked with a strange symbol on the cover. The pages were brittle and yellowed by time. I nearly put it back where I'd found it, afraid that it would crumble in my hands, but something about the symbol on the cover drew me. Checking to make sure I was still alone, I settled in a comfortable chair near the window overlooking the river and carefully opened it to the first page. My heart raced, terrified that I might be trespassing on old family secrets, but I couldn't resist the pull of curiosity. Something about this book, however, made me both curious and uncomfortable as the pages crinkled between my fingers. The writing was faded and barely legible. I held the book closer to the lamp and cautiously turned a few pages until I finally came across a sprawled passage that I was able to make out.

The witch sought revenge upon the Bardon's for their deceit and betrayal. One night, while the Lady Bardon was away to visit her sister, the witch crept inside the castle walls, using the dark of night as a cloak to conceal her bent and hunchbacked form. She silently creeped up the stairs and made her way to the Lord's bedchamber whilst he slept. Inside, she cast a glamour upon herself, transforming into the Lord's beautiful wife and climbed into bed with him.

Believing that his beloved had returned from her trip early, the Lord made love to the witch. After which, in the pre-dawn hours, the witch escaped the castle in possession of his seed. It is believed that it is with that intimate ingredient that she placed her curse.

Days later, the Lord's temper became extreme. His eyes bulged with madness. Lady Bardon returned from her trip to find her kind and gentle husband greatly altered. Upon the suggestion that a physician might tend him, Lord Bardon's madness possessed him fully. During a sojourn along the river, he grabbed his wife by the shoulders and with inhuman strength, lifted her high above his head and threw her in the racing waters. Weighted down by her skirts, Lady Bardon was no match for the currents and was tragically swept beneath the waves.

When the Lord's servants tried to subdue his Lordship, he ripped at their flesh with his fingers. Fingers that had curled into talons. His skin blackened and cracked. His beady eyes reddened with a demonic light, and his legs bowed into great, beast-like haunches. Horns grew from his head. With his transformation nigh complete, two dozen men joined forces and might to subdue the Bardon Beast.

I gasped, riveted, and horrified by the tale the writer had described. I turned several more pages, hoping to discover why the witch had cursed Lord Bardon, until I found a few sentences that I could barely make out. I squinted, bringing the book closer to my face as I continued to read.

To this day, the line of Bardon men, upon the first signs of transformation, must kill themselves or risk killing those they love most. No cure has ever been found, nor the witch and her purpose discovered.

I stared at those last lines until their image burned into my brain. I hadn't spent much time with the Bardon's, but the description of Lord Bardon's early symptoms matched what I had seen in the late Lord Bardon before his death. I chewed my bottom lip. It was probably nothing, I tried to convince myself as blood rushed to my head. A fable meant to warn future Bardon's of dealing with witches. There was no truth to this book. There couldn't be. Witches, and demonic beasts, and curses... none of that is real. Lord Bardon likely shared some genetic traits with his ancestor that the writer used to make his tale even more convincing. Still, no matter what I told myself, my heart refused to settle. I feared for my friend. Not even my power as a Princess and heir to the throne of Britain could save Charles if this curse was true.

"Gwen? Gwen, where are you?" I heard my maid in the hallway and shoved the book behind a cushion before the door opened.

"There you are, Your Highness. Lord Bardon was looking for you. He has a visitor and wishes for you to join him in the front parlour." Brigid bowed respectfully as she stepped into the library.

Nine years ago, we were sent here to live with the Bardon's while my father worked tirelessly to stabilize the country and reinforce our borders. Forced together, we'd long since dispensed with formalities and titles. Brigid was as much my friend as Charles, and I dropped my pretence of reading the magazine I'd found on the nearby table, frowning as I looked at her.

"What's wrong Brigid? Why are you concerned about this visitor?" I asked.

"He's been sent by your father," Brigid hurriedly whispered. "A man with bright green eyes that seem to see right through to your very soul. I think he might be here to take us home."

"Home," I whispered longingly. Bardon Rock had become my home these past years and I scarcely remembered the opulent palace in the heart of London where I spent my early childhood. I wanted nothing more than to return to my home and my father's arms, but the knowledge that my best friend might be cursed for eternity tore at me. I couldn't go home without doing everything I could to protect him from himself.

"I'm sorry Brigid," I replied sadly. "But we're not going anywhere."

I rose from the chair, ignoring my maid's open-mouthed expression and determinedly strode past her. My running shoes squeaked on the marble floors as I ran through the halls in search of Charles and this mysterious visitor. I found them in the sitting room, the door crashing into the wall behind me as I barged inside. Charles looked up from his letter, surprised and gaping at me before remembering we weren't alone. Setting his shoulders back, he rose from his chair and bowed formally. His face donning a mask of neutrality, as a lock of his fair hair fell over his forehead. I hated the wariness in his normally warm, brown eyes and turned away from him, hoping to dull the ache that had begun to bloom in the pit of my stomach. It was clear that he had already resolved himself to the idea of my leaving.

"Your Highness," Charles nodded respectfully at the man standing next to him. "Allow me to introduce you to Pollux. He's been sent by your father to bring you home and act as your bodyguard. It would seem his brother, Castor is no longer enough to protect you."

My eyes locked with Pollux's bright green ones, and my heart skipped. Sandy brown hair framed his chiseled features and brushed his broad shoulders. The cockiness in his arched brow took my breath away when it should have had the opposite affect. I hated cocky men, they always underestimated me.

"Your Highness," he half-bowed. "Please call me Paul."

I nodded, ignoring the inquisitive look Charles was giving me.

"Paul," I tested his name. "I have no wish to leave, and no need of an additional bodyguard. Cas has been quite effective in that regard."

"There is a greater need then you realized, Your Highness. We will stay if we can, but I fear your location here is no longer safe. *An dorchadas*, the Darkling, has discovered your general whereabouts. It's only a matter of time before he finds you." Paul's voice washed soothingly over me, and I nearly forgot my earlier determination to save my friend.

"I'm needed here," I replied, steel lacing my tone as I fought against this strange hold, he already had over me.

"My Lord, may we have a moment alone?" Paul turned to Charles and asked.

"Of course," Charles nodded and instead of heading for the door, he stepped over to me and wrapped his arms around me.

"It will be alright, Gwen. You'll see," he whispered soothingly in my ear. I kissed his cheek and hugged him close before letting him go.

The door clicked closed behind him with a quiet click that echoed through the room. With Charles gone, I was completely alone with this strange and beautiful man. I watched him warily as he stared at the closed door.

"Your Highness, it is not safe here," he began, and I cut him off with a wave.

"It was safe enough for the last nine years. Charles needs me, and I won't leave him."

"Your boyfriend can fend for himself."

"No, he can't," I whispered as Paul stalked closer to me. He took a lock of my hair and wrapped it around his fingers, tugging gently to force me to look into his eyes once more.

"Why?" He asked calmly.

I desperately wanted to keep what I had learned a secret, but there was something about him that had me opening to him unexpectedly. My words came rushing out, before I could stop them. Paul listened intently as I explained the curse on the Bardons.

"Come with me, and I will help you find a way to save your friend," he replied when I finished.

I don't know what it was about him, but I believed him. Our eyes locked, I slowly nodded in agreement. I would go with him, but I would make sure he held up his end of the bargain.

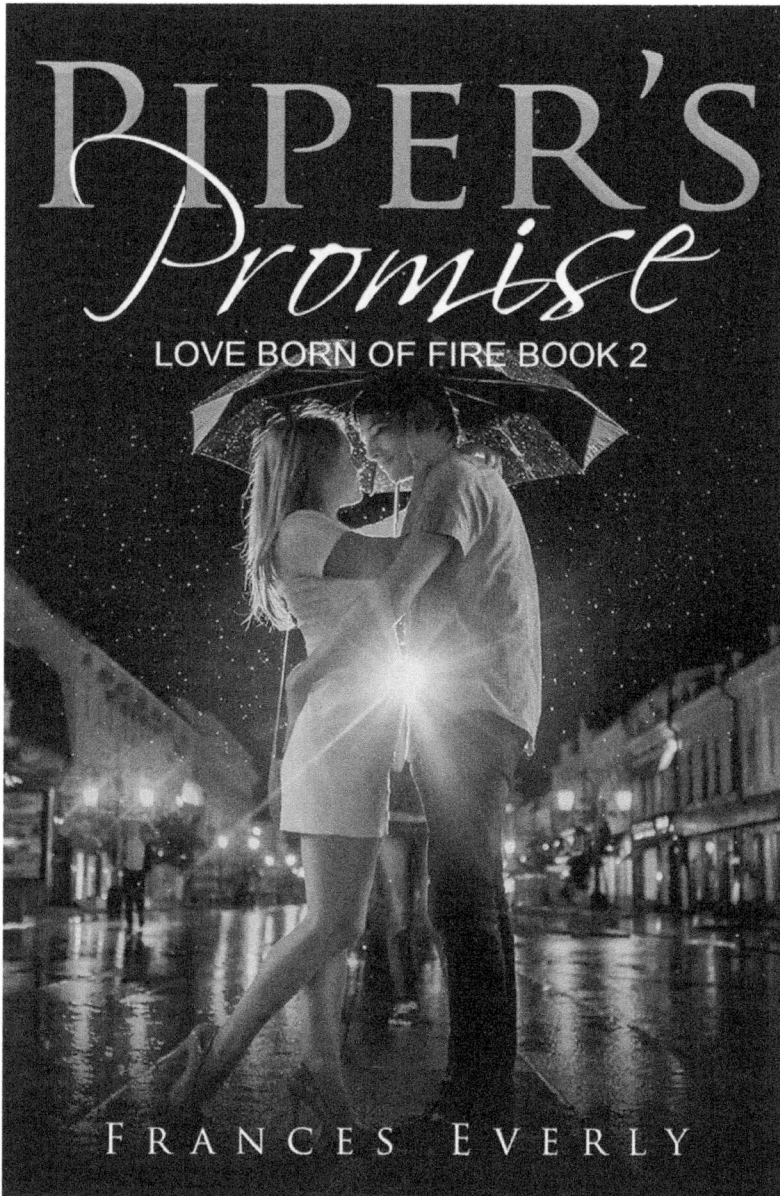

PIPER'S Promise

LOVE BORN OF FIRE BOOK 2

FRANCES EVERLY

FRANCES EVERLY

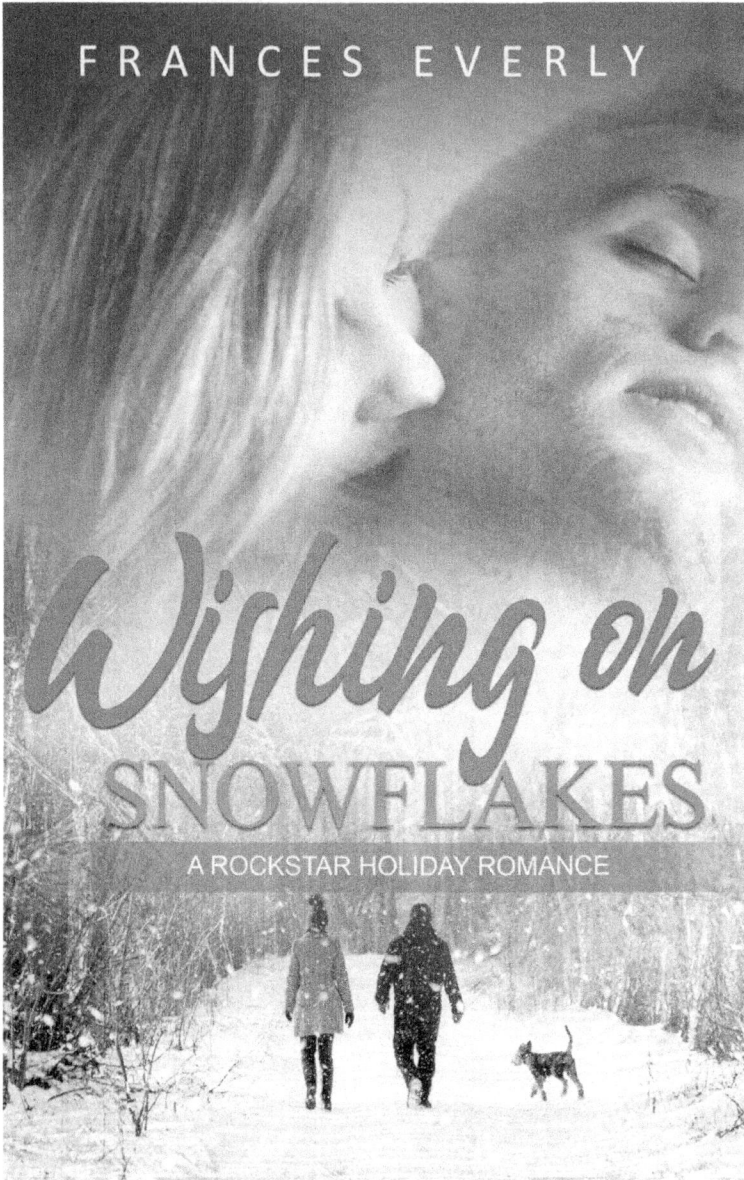

Wishing on SNOWFLAKES

A ROCKSTAR HOLIDAY ROMANCE

Made in the USA
Las Vegas, NV
16 December 2021